ESCAPE IN DARKNESS

ESCAPE IN DARKNESS

Kathleen Fidler

Illustrated by Geoffrey Whittam

CANONGATE • KELPIES

First published 1961 by Lutterworth Press
First published in Kelpies in 1987

Cover illustration by Alexa Rutherford

Printed in Great Britain
by Cox and Wyman Ltd, Reading, Berkshire

ISBN 0 86241 157 2

For
KATHLEEN HELEN McTAGGART
With My Dearest Love

CANONGATE PUBLISHING LTD
17 JEFFREY STREET, EDINBURGH EH1 1DR

Contents

INTRODUCTION

In 1600 a strange adventure befell King James VI of Scotland, who later became James I of England. James was just about to set off hunting from Falkland Palace when the brother of the Earl of Gowrie, Alexander Ruthven, came riding up in great haste and told the King a mysterious story about a strange man with a pot of gold whom he had found in Perth. He begged the King to come with him to see this man at Gowrie House in Perth. James was always a greedy, grasping man, and he went with him.

At Gowrie House, Alexander Ruthven led the King up a spiral stair and through several rooms. Suddenly James found himself confronted by an armed man. Ruthven threatened to kill the King if he uttered a cry, and, leaving the armed man to guard him, he went away to fetch his brother, the Earl of Gowrie. When the King rushed to a window and opened it, the armed man found he did not dare kill the King. Just then Alexander Ruthven returned. The King's attendants were just leaving Gowrie House, thinking the King had gone, when James thrust his head out of the window with Ruthven's hand at his throat. He managed to shout, "Treason! Help! Help!"

His men rushed back into the house, battered their way into the room and slew Alexander Ruthven. John Ruthven, the Earl of Gowrie, appeared with his followers and, in the fight that followed, the Earl was slain.

No one quite knows the truth of what really happened. The King said the Ruthvens meant to kidnap and kill him. Many people thought the King made up the whole conspiracy to get rid of the Ruthvens whom he hated. Even after they were dead he had their bodies taken from the ground and tried, then hung, drawn and quartered.

The Earl of Gowrie's two younger brothers, Patrick and William, fled to England, but the King's unforgiving spirit pursued them even there, and when James became King of England, too, Patrick was made a prisoner in the Tower of London. William managed to escape to the continent and all trace of him was lost. Even the Earl of Gowrie's two sisters, Beatrix and Barbara, who were the Queen's ladies-in-waiting, were driven from the court into hiding.

James deprived the Ruthvens of all their lands. He never forgot his hatred of them. "I will stamp out the name of Ruthven for ever!" he declared.

CHAPTER 1

THE DUEL

It was the year 1613.

The clashing swords glinted red in the slanting rays of the newly risen sun. Ankle-deep in a marshy meadow near the Dutch town of Bergen-op-Zoom, the two young men cut and thrust and parried, pressing hard upon each other. It was a breathless August day and the white silk shirts of the fighters clung stickily to their backs. Half screened by a clump of trees to which their horses were tethered, the two seconds and the two doctors watched the fighters, their faces grim and apprehensive.

Sir John Heidon, Sir Edward Sackville's second, shaded his eyes the better to follow the quick play of the swords and he shook his head. "I fear me this quarrel is too deep to be settled with a little blood-letting."

John Crawford pressed his lips together. "Lord Kinloss has told me that only Sir Edward Sackville's life will satisfy him for the insult Sir Edward put upon him."

"Watch now!" Sir John exclaimed. "Oh! Oh!"

Sackville had lunged forward at his enemy, but his thrust was short and Lord Kinloss's rapier gashed his arm and the sleeve of the white silk shirt rapidly became crimson. Sackville's wound only maddened him the more and he pressed harder upon Lord Kinloss. Again he lunged and missed, and this time Lord Kinloss struck hard towards his heart. Sackville quickly parried, and though he could not avoid the thrust, he deflected it upwards. The sword stabbed him in the right shoulder, but still he went on fighting. Yet another blow almost sliced off his little finger, but he still gripped his sword.

Again, fighting up and down, lunging and recovering, each strove to get inside the other's guard. Then, by one of those strange chances of duelling, the point of each thin blade got entangled in the basket-like silver hilt of the other, and neither man could release his sword and strike.

"Quit your swords, both of you!" Sir John Heidon cried.

"Drop your swords and begin the fight over again, if you must," Crawford suggested, but neither man would let go his sword.

"What? And let him run me through if I quit my hold?" Lord Kinloss panted.

"Not when he has sworn to kill me!" Sackville retorted.

They both struggled to free their rapiers, tugging hard. At last Sackville gave a violent wrench to his weapon, grasping the other's blade in his gloved hand as he did so, and freed the point of his sword. At once he laid it at Kinloss's throat, still keeping his grip of Kinloss's weapon.

"Beg for your life, or yield up your sword to me," he demanded.

"Never! I will die first!" Kinloss declared.

"Then die! It is you or I for it!" Sackville panted and struck at Kinloss's heart.

Kinloss twisted his body and, though the thrust did not reach his heart, it passed between his ribs and he staggered. Quick as lightning Sir Edward Sackville withdrew his sword and struck hard again and this time his sword passed through the body of Kinloss, who clapped his hand to his left side.

"Oh, I am slain!" he gasped, but with all the dying force left in him, he lunged yet again at Sackville from whose wounds the blood streamed.

Sackville gave a desperate heave and tumbled Lord Kinloss upon his back, falling with him to the ground. Quickly he pulled himself to his knees beside his foe. "Ask your life now and I will spare it," he offered.

Pale to his lips, Kinloss still shook his head. "I scorn to ask it!" His eyes dazed, he groped round for his sword and tried again to rise. Sackville, fearing Kinloss even in death, pushed him back again and held him down.

Lord Kinloss's surgeon rushed from the clump of trees. "He will bleed to death if his wounds are not stopped at once," he cried.

"Do you wish your surgeon to come?" Sackville asked Kinloss.

Lord Kinloss nodded, and both surgeons rushed to the aid of their masters. Sackville's surgeon was just in time to catch him in his arms as he fainted from loss of blood.

Lord Kinloss lay white and gasping on the turf, but his eyes still stared wildly round. It was plain that little could be done for him. From his wounds the life was ebbing fast. His surgeon did what he could, his face working with pity and love, then, as if driven mad by the sight, he seized Kinloss's sword and rushed upon Sackville. "You wicked man! You shall die, too!" he cried. He might have stabbed Sackville to the heart, but a cry from his dying master, "Rascal, hold thy hand!" stopped him. The other surgeon sprang to his feet, snatching Sackville's sword, and prepared to defend him.

"Drop your swords, you wretches! Has there not been enough bloodshed?" Crawford cried, rushing towards them. "Look to your masters!"

It was plain that little could be done for Lord Kinloss. His wounds had gone too deep. He beckoned to Crawford. "John! John!" Crawford sank on his knees beside him.

"I have not long," Kinloss whispered in a faint voice. "Tell—tell Elizabeth—to take my heart to Culross Abbey. My heart has always been in Scotland. Send word, too, to carry out the work my father started there—to build a hospital in our memory. . . ." His voice faltered and he rested a moment, closing his eyes.

"I will take your message to your wife, my lord," Crawford promised.

Suddenly Lord Kinloss opened his eyes very wide and made a last tremendous effort. "Bid Elizabeth take the boy—our son—to Culross, to George Bruce, my kinsman there. He will look to him and see right done. Give Elizabeth my ring for the boy—and tell Elizabeth—tell Elizabeth—she had all my love to the last." His voice grew so faint that Crawford had to put his ear to Kinloss's mouth to catch the last few words.

"I will carry your words faithfully to her," he promised.

Kinloss closed his eyes and nodded, then he gave one long shuddering gasp and was gone. John Crawford stumbled to his feet, his eyes misted with tears. He crossed to the other little group now trying to hoist Sir Edward Sackville upon his horse. "Sir!" he addressed Sackville. "My friend, Lord Edward Bruce, is dead by your hand."

Sackville turned paler still. "Had I not killed him, he would have killed me. It was he who challenged me to fight him. I have letters to prove it."

"It was your insult to him and to his lady that provoked this quarrel. Did you not breathe slander against him in the ear of King James?"

Sackville looked guilty and shifted his eyes from those of his accuser and did not answer.

"The Bruces are not slow to revenge, remember, but the vengeance of God is even swifter," Crawford told him, then turned his back on him. Sackville left the field, escorted by Sir John Heidon and his surgeon. Not long afterwards a farm cart bore the body of Edward Bruce, Lord Kinloss, to the church of Bergen-op-Zoom, and Crawford rode south to bear the doleful tidings to Lady Kinloss.

A week later John Crawford reached Paris. As soon as he had made his arrangements at an inn, he rode out to the suburb of Neuilly. There, at a tall narrow house in a quiet square, he handed his horse to his groom, then paused with his hand on the knocker as though unwilling to break the peace of the square with a harsh tattoo. He dreaded the task of breaking the sad news to Elizabeth Bruce. He remembered her, gay and charming, beside Lord Kinloss at many stately balls at the court of the French king. That was before Edward Sackville breathed poison into King James's ear that his favourite courtier, Lord Kinloss, had entered into an alliance with a woman who was a Ruthven and that the King could trust him no more. That was the slander that brought about the fateful duel.

Once again Crawford stretched out his hand to the knocker, but just as he did so, the door was plucked open, and a stout middle-aged woman with grey hair stood before him. She wore the full linen apron over her grey dress and the close-fitting cap with wings that betokened a serving woman. She looked with alarm at Crawford.

"You are alone, sir? You have come back alone?" she faltered.

"Aye, Nan, I have." There was no mistaking the sorrow in his voice.

"He—he—Lord Kinloss—is he grievously wounded?"

"Worse than that, Nan."

"Oh, no, no!" she wailed. "Little did we think when we

watched the two of you ride away that it would come to this! Oh, the bonnie man he was! However will my lady bear it!"

"Alas, I have come to break the news to her. Will you ask her to see me, please?"

Nan hesitated. "She—she is not well, sir. All day she has not said a word, nor has a bite of food passed her lips. Lady Barbara Ruthven is with her now. She will have no one else. Perhaps you should speak with Lady Barbara first."

Nan Cranston led the way up the stairs to a room on the first floor overlooking the garden at the back of the house. She tapped gently on the door. It was opened by Barbara Ruthven, tall, black-haired, with large dark eyes, a woman of striking dignity. She, too, went pale when she saw John Crawford was alone.

"My Lord Kinloss, what of him?" she asked, in a quick, quiet voice.

John Crawford gave a sad gesture with his hands. "Slain! Sir Edward Sackville ran him through. He died in my arms, but not before he had given me messages for the Lady Elizabeth."

Barbara Ruthven swayed a little, but grasped the door-post and steadied herself. "What have you done with his body?"

"He is buried in the church of Bergen-op-Zoom, but my lord left certain instructions about other matters——"

"We must break these ill-tidings to Lady Elizabeth as best we can. She—she has lain there all day with curtains drawn, moaning. Ever since dawn she has had terrible forebodings."

"Aye, aye! She swore she saw a death's head in the glass," Nan Cranston, still standing beside them, shook her head woefully. Barbara Ruthven threw her a reproving glance, for Nan took a liberty in speaking, as many old servants will.

"That may have been the wandering of a sick fancy, but it is plain that more ails her than this terrible fear for Lord Kinloss. When terror and sickness are joined together, then indeed we must be careful lest the shock be too great for her. Come with me, sir, and together we will try to ease the blow, if that be possible. Go you, Nan, and look to the child," she dismissed Nan who still hovered about the door.

She closed the door gently behind them and together they approached the large four-poster bed with its silken hangings. Gently Barbara Ruthven parted the curtains.

On the bed lay Elizabeth Bruce, her eyes wild and staring. She started up when she saw John Crawford, then fell back weakly on the bed.

"It is not Edward. Water! Water, Barbara! For the love of heaven!" she gasped.

"Here is a better drink than water, my lassie," Barbara said tenderly, pouring a pale green liquid into a goblet from a jug. "It has the juice of many healing herbs. Drink this, now."

Elizabeth drank the long cool draught. "Thank you, Barbara. You are good to me." She fell back exhausted on the bed and closed her eyes. Barbara laid her hand on her forehead.

"She is very fevered," she told Crawford.

"She looks ill indeed," John Crawford agreed.

At the sound of the strange voice Elizabeth opened her eyes again and peered at him. "Who is that? Who is that in the shadows?" she cried. "Is he the doctor?"

"No, Elizabeth, he is not the doctor. He is a friend—a friend of Edward's. He has brought you a message."

"I am John Crawford, at your service, mistress," he told her.

The herbal drink seemed to have revived Elizabeth a little. She stared at him as if trying to piece understanding together. "John Crawford? Edward's friend?" she muttered. Then her memory suddenly cleared and a spasm of fear shot across her face. "But Edward rode away with you to—to Holland some days ago. Oh, if only this terrible pain in my head would let me think!"

There was vinegar standing in a bowl on the nearby table and Barbara squeezed out a cloth in it and placed it on the girl's throbbing temples.

"That is easier." Memory suddenly came flooding in to her consciousness. "Edward? Edward? He went to fight a duel with Sackville. Is he not with you?" She started up again in fear.

Crawford shook his head unhappily. "No, my lady."

"Where is he, then? Where is he?" she cried wildly.

Crawford sought to put off the evil moment when he must tell her the truth. "He has sent messages to you, together with this ring that he bade me to take from his finger."

"Messages? His ring? But why has he not come himself?"

"Alas, madam, he cannot come."

His meaning began to penetrate even her clouded mind.

"Cannot come? He has sent me his ring? But he would only do that if—if——" Her voice faltered. "He is not dead?" she cried.

The stricken look on Crawford's face and Barbara's muttered prayer, "Peace be with his soul," told her the truth.

A terrible pallor overspread Elizabeth's face. Her eyes closed and her whole body shook with a violent shuddering. Barbara seized her and held her tight in her arms. "There, my bairn! There!" she said with tenderness. She signed to Crawford to pour water into a cup, then, from the pocket that hung at her waist, she took a tiny phial and dropped three drops from it into the water. It turned the red of wine. Crawford watched her curiously. He remembered what had been said of the Ruthven family, that they knew magic and dabbled in the Black Arts, but that they were skilled in medicine, too.

Barbara held the glass to Elizabeth's lips and forced a sip of the draught through her chattering teeth. Another sip or two and the moaning died away and the intense shuddering ceased.

"Listen, Elizabeth! Edward sent messages to you by Mr. Crawford. Will you not hear them, my dear?"

Elizabeth nodded.

"My Lord Kinloss asked that a hospital should be built in Culross, for old people who are poor, that his memory might live."

"It shall be done." Elizabeth's voice was very faint.

"He bade you to take the boy, James Bruce, your son, to his kinsman, George Bruce, at Culross. He said that George Bruce would look to the lad and see right was done by him."

"The boy has not to go then to Edward's brother, Thomas?" Barbara Ruthven put in a quick question.

Crawford shook his head. "I do not believe he had enough trust in Thomas."

Barbara was quick to understand. "If it were not for his child, James Bruce, then Thomas would be Lord Kinloss's heir." She cast a troubled glance at Elizabeth, whose strength seemed to be flagging again. "We will speak more of this later. Are there other messages yet? And the ring, if you please, while she still understands you."

Crawford bent over Elizabeth and slipped a ring over her finger. "He sent this ring to you for the boy, and he bade me tell you that you had all his love to the last."

"As he has mine." The words were almost too faint to be heard.

"There was one thing more. Though his body must rest in an alien land, he wished his heart to be taken to Scotland and buried there in Culross Abbey."

Barbara answered for Elizabeth. "It shall be done. I will see to it for her. She cannot stand any more now. Will you, for the love you had for him, arrange for a casket to be made to hold his heart? I cannot visit the silversmiths while she is so ill."

"Leave these matters to me. I will see to them," Crawford promised.

Suddenly Elizabeth gave a great cry. "He is gone! Edward is gone!" and fell back unconscious upon the bed.

"Fetch Nan to me quickly, I beg you," Barbara said. "This is more than the shock of sorrow. There is a fever of the brain, too. Nan is in the room below this one."

Crawford went in search of the old nurse. He heard the sound of a Highland lullaby in the ground-floor room and found Nan rocking a cradle.

"Please go to the Lady Barbara at once," he said. When Nan scuttled hurriedly up the stairs, he bent over the cradle and looked at the lovely child with the rosy flush of sleep in his cheeks.

"Poor lad! What is to come to you with your father killed and you half a Ruthven, with the blood of that unlucky, ill-fated family coursing in your veins?" Shaking his head, he let himself out of the door.

Ten days later John Crawford called again to visit Barbara Ruthven. This time he carried with him a square wooden box. Nan Cranston escorted him to the parlour where Lord Kinloss's son, James Bruce, lay in his cradle. As she eyed the box that Crawford carried, her old eyes filled with tears, but saying only, "Will you be seated, sir. Lady Barbara will be with you in a few minutes," she withdrew.

When Barbara Ruthven entered the room she looked pale and tired. Crawford rose and made a low bow.

"Mistress, I have brought you that which I promised, the casket containing the heart of my friend, Lord Kinloss." He opened the wooden box and inside, on a lining of velvet, rested a heart-shaped casket of silver. It bore a coat of arms, that of the Kinloss family, with their motto, *Fuimus*.

Barbara Ruthven looked at the silver casket with tears in her eyes. "Poor Edward! Poor Elizabeth! A pity that all their love should end like this!"

"There is still the child," Crawford reminded her gently. "What will become of him now?"

"I shall look to him, for I am his near kinswoman," Lady Barbara replied. "I will be father and mother to him now he has neither."

"I know Lady Elizabeth was a Ruthven by birth, and therefore kin to you, but how near kin was she to the Earl of Gowrie?"

Barbara Ruthven hesitated. "Edward Kinloss trusted you, John Crawford, so I may do so, too. Elizabeth was the daughter of my brother John, the Earl of Gowrie."

Crawford started in astonishment. "But it was said the Earl was not married at his death."

"It was *said*, perhaps, but only a few people knew the truth of that. My brother was a student at Padua in Italy from the age of fifteen till he was almost twenty years old."

"Aye, so I have heard, and that while he was there, he dabbled in magic."

"He learned some arts of medicine," she replied briefly. "What people did not know was that he made a secret marriage with the daughter of one of his tutors. Not a wise marriage, maybe, but who is wise when young and in love?" She smiled a little sadly. "Lady Elizabeth was the child of that marriage. She was my niece. John and I were always close friends, and I was the only one he told of his foolish marriage and of the child."

"You too were at King James's court in Edinburgh, were you not?"

"Yes, I and my sister Beatrix were two of the Queen's ladies. When the King accused my brothers of conspiring against his life and they were both slain at the point of the sword at Gowrie House, then we had to leave the court. King James's vengeance was hot against the Ruthvens. He declared he would wipe out our family; that no one should ever bear our name again. I and my younger brothers, Patrick and William, fled to

England, for Queen Elizabeth was alive then and gave us refuge."

"But when Queen Elizabeth died and James became King of England too, then you would no longer be safe," Crawford said.

"No. King James sought us out again for vengeance. Patrick he caught and he is still a prisoner in the Tower of London, but William and I escaped to Paris. It was while I lived here that I had a fancy to send for the Earl of Gowrie's child from Italy, that I might have the child of my dead brother. Her family willingly gave her up to me. I brought her up quietly here in Paris as my young kinswoman."

"Was it in Paris that Lord Kinloss saw her first?"

"It was at a ball given by the Vicomte de Malines, her very first ball, and she was sixteen and very lovely. They fell in love at first sight, and Lord Kinloss came to ask my permission to marry her. It was then that I told him that she was a Ruthven, and whose daughter she was."

For a moment silence fell between Barbara Ruthven and Lord Crawford.

"Lord Kinloss was King James's favourite courtier," John Crawford said softly.

"I knew that, and I knew that James would never forgive him if he married a Ruthven, the daughter of his dead enemy. Had not the King vowed to root us out, so that our name should never be spoken in Scotland again?" Lady Barbara said bitterly. "I warned him and advised him to go back to England and give himself time to consider the matter."

"And he would not?"

Barbara shook her head. "No. There were never two people more desperately in love, and Kinloss feared to lose her if he went back to England without marrying her first. 'The King will come round in time,' Kinloss declared. But there could be no question of a *public* marriage, unless he wished to make an enemy of King James for ever. So the two of them were married secretly, Scots' fashion."

"You mean they declared themselves man and wife, in the presence of witnesses?"

"Yes, that is all our Scottish law demands to make a marriage legal, that they should take hands and make their vows before two witnesses."

"Who were the witnesses?" he asked.

"Nan Cranston and I. Nan had been nurse in my family at Perth and I sent for her to come to Paris to look after Elizabeth when she was a small child."

John Crawford looked troubled. "It might have been better if there had been other witnesses, not of the Ruthven family alone."

"No doubt you are right, but the marriage had to be kept secret till Kinloss could make his peace with King James first."

Crawford shook his head. "James would never have forgiven Kinloss for his marriage with the daughter of one who had been his greatest enemy, especially when the King still feared the vengeance of the Ruthven family."

"I think Edward Kinloss realized that, for he lingered on in Paris and kept putting off the day when he should go to England and acquaint the King with what he had done. Then the child was born and that was another reason for delaying."

"And that gave Kinloss's enemy, Sir Edward Sackville, a chance to whisper in the King's ear that Kinloss was living with a Ruthven and conspiring with the King's enemies. He hinted at a base plot to murder James and that Kinloss was in it up to the hilt," Crawford told her.

"So that was why Edward fought Sackville? He would fear to tell Elizabeth that their marriage had ruined him with the King. All he said was that Sackville had lied about him to King James. I could well understand that he could not let that slander go unchallenged by his sword," Barbara said proudly.

"You see, the King still fears that William Ruthven might avenge his brother, the Earl of Gowrie's death, and no one knows where William Ruthven is. It was rumoured that he was here with you in Paris." Crawford looked narrowly at her.

"He was," she admitted, "But he is here no longer. King James had too many spies in Paris. Where William is now, I am not at liberty to tell you." She pressed her lips together.

The baby in the cradle gave a whimper, then settled down to sleep again.

"What will you do with the casket?" Crawford asked.

"It is the child's right to take his father's heart back to Culross in Scotland, but he is too small yet, poor little mite. But one day he will be grown enough, and when that day comes, James Bruce shall bear Kinloss's heart to Culross and claim his rights there to his father's lands. Now he is motherless, too, I will see to that," Barbara Ruthven tossed her head proudly.

Crawford puckered his brows as if in sudden doubt. He bent over the cradle and gently stroked the cheeks of the sleeping baby. "There are some years to run before he will be old enough to do that. I beg you to remember, mistress, that this child is half a Ruthven, and King James has sworn to root out the Ruthven family, tree and branch. My advice to you is to live with him quietly in some place on the Continent, where the King's hand cannot reach out and strike at this bairn."

Barbara Ruthven clasped her hands and her knuckles were white. Then quietly she replied, "It might be wise to do as you say. I thank you for all you have done for us, John Crawford. It shall not be forgotten." She dropped him a gracious curtsy and held out her hand.

"If ever I can be of service to you, madam, you have only to command me," he assured her, as he bent over her hand. A moment later he was gone.

Barbara Ruthven bent over the child in the cradle. "I will be both father and mother to you, James Bruce," she vowed.

CHAPTER 2

RETURN TO CULROSS

ELEVEN years had passed since Edward Bruce, Lord Kinloss, had fought his duel with Sir Edward Sackville and lost his life. It was the year 1624. During those eleven years his son James Bruce had been brought up by Barbara Ruthven. They had left Paris and dwelt in many cities of Europe, Rome, Vienna, Heidelburg, Leiden, Padua. Lady Barbara had seen to it that the boy was well-schooled in all the arts that became a gentleman. He spoke several languages with ease. He could read with understanding in Latin and French and Italian, and already he could make pretty play with a sword. Then, when the days drew near to his twelfth birthday, she looked at the lad with pride and said, "The time has come at last, James. We will go back to Scotland."

A small ship beat her way up the Firth of Forth in the teeth of a late summer storm that blew white caps on the crests of all the grey waves. She was a squat Dutch ship, broad in the beam, but sturdily built. She rounded Hound Point and her skipper sailed her skilfully past the half-submerged rock of Inchgarrie and beat north-westwards into the shelter of the bay of Saint Margaret's Hope.

Heedless of the blown spume, Barbara Ruthven and James Bruce stood in the forepeak of the ship, holding fast by the foremast as the ship lifted and fell with the waves. Barbara wore a dark woollen cloak over her dress of black velvet, with its tight-fitted, richly ornamented bodice and full skirt, while James was dressed in a dark green doublet and hose, a small lace ruff about his neck, and a short cape hanging from his shoulders.

"Here are the shores of Fife at last. Soon we shall sail into Torry Bay and across the water you will see the red roofs of Culross," Barbara Ruthven told the boy. As if to mock her words the dark curtain of the rain came down between them and the northern shore of the Firth.

Still the *Hans Pieter* tacked her way up the Forth estuary, the skipper taking his bearings from landmarks on the south, the castle of Blackness and the rocky point of Borrowstoneness beyond. Then, as if relenting, the weather suddenly cleared; the sun shone from behind white galleons of cloud and the grey waters of the Firth became sparkling blue.

"It is aye like this in Scotland," Barbara told James. "One minute it will be raining and the next the sun will be burning you, and the best of the summer days will take a sudden chill in the evenings when the haar drifts in from the sea and blots out every place."

"The haar?" James asked.

"The sea mist. It is a Scandinavian word that comes from our Scottish trade with the seaboard countries across the North Sea, and so we borrow words from each other. You will be surprised at the many ships from the Continent that you will find at Culross."

The ship was hugging closer to the northern shore and a wide shallow bay opened before them. Near the shore was a small island, and, between the island and the shore, the sea was filled with craft riding at anchor before a small town. Above the shore the ground rose in terraces bright with gardens and orchards stretching up to the walls of a ruined abbey and an old church with a square tower. To the left of the church, hidden largely by trees, stood a fine house. Behind and above all lay the dark blue hills.

"Look yonder! There is Culross and your home," Barbara Ruthven exclaimed, a catch in her voice.

James stared without speaking for a moment, and his aunt threw him an anxious glance. Was the boy going to be disappointed after all? Then from James came a cry, "Oh, it is beautiful, beautiful! I had no thought it would look like this."

Barbara Ruthven caught him suddenly to her. "Pray God it will be friendly to you as well as beautiful, for Scotland has not always been kind to the Ruthvens."

The *Hans Pieter* turned in towards the shore; the sails were slackened and came rattling down and were quickly furled, and the sailors took to the long sweeps, as the great oars were called, and brought the ship in to the landing quay.

James Bruce stared about him in wonderment. All along the shore, especially where poor cottages backed on to the beach, fires burned with a strange blue light, and from great iron cauldrons slung on tripods above them rose steamy vapours. Barefooted men and women in sodden dirty rags tended the fires.

"Whatever are those people doing? They look like witches crouched over horrid brews," James said.

"They are making salt from the sea water," Barbara Ruthven told him. "Culross does a great trade in salt, both to pickle the herring and salmon, and to salt the beef."

"Oh!" James exclaimed, staring at a group of men working a boat alongside them in the tiny harbour. "Are the inhabitants of Culross *black*-faced?"

Barbara laughed aloud. "What a bairn you are! Those are the men who mine the coal hereabouts. Colliers, they are called. Their faces are black with coal-dust, not by nature."

"Do they never wash?" James asked in surprise.

"Yes, before they go to church on the Sabbath," Barbara chuckled. "I expect they work for your cousin, George Bruce. He owns the coal mines of Culross."

James was still staring about him. "What is that queer kind of place in the middle of the water, like a small island with a great wall round it?" he asked curiously.

"I am not sure. It is so many years since I was in Scotland. Perhaps it is some work of Sir George Bruce's." She turned to the skipper and asked him a question.

"*Ja, ja!*" he nodded. "Coal-mine. Under-water coal-mine. Belong Sir at big house."

"An under-water mine? Does that mean it goes under the sea?" James Bruce's eyes sparkled with excitement.

"*Ja.* Under the sea," the Dutchman confirmed. "Coal come from tunnels under the sea." He pointed, "Big wheel there keeps it drained."

"Shall I be able to go down and explore the mine?" James asked his aunt eagerly.

She smiled. "That will be for Sir George Bruce to say, James. Come now, though. The ship has been made fast to the quay. It's time we went ashore. Can you spare two of your men to carry our boxes?" she asked the skipper.

He nodded, and they stepped across a gangplank on to the quay. Barbara Ruthven paused a little uncertainly. She looked across a wide kind of square with houses along three sides of it and one side open to the sea. Lanes led off from the square between gaps in the houses. On the far side two great houses stood back from the square. They were built at right angles to each other, and one was quite a new house. They were both enclosed in the same courtyard with a low wall, facing the quay. Barbara spoke to a shoreman unloading cargo from the *Hans Pieter*.

"One of those houses belongs to Sir George Bruce, does it not? It is some years since I was last in Culross."

"Aye, mistress. Both houses belong to Sir George. He built the second house for his large family. They sleep there and have their private quarters. The old house he keeps mainly for entertaining his guests and the family eat there. From there, too, he conducts his business."

She turned to the men carrying their boxes across the gangplank. "Follow us to the great house on the left."

James looked puzzled. "Why is there no one to meet us?"

His aunt looked a little troubled. "They do not know that we were coming in the ship. I—I had not sent a letter. A letter costs so much to send, and you know we have little money and must use it carefully."

The boy nodded. Barbara Ruthven did not tell him the real reason, that she was not sure if they would be welcome. Sir George Bruce stood high in King James's favour, and he might not be too pleased to give hospitality to anyone of the Ruthven name, for fear of offending the King. For a moment she glanced doubtfully at the two formidable stone houses, and then, squaring her shoulders, and with her head held high, she led the way through the gate and up the flight of shallow stone steps to the house on the left. Barbara Ruthven hesitated, not knowing quite how to announce their arrival. Then she looked for the tirling-pin, a kind of giant iron corkscrew with a ring attached, which hung outside Scottish houses.

"Will you tirl at the pin, please, James? It is on your side of the door."

The lad looked bewildered. "I don't know what you mean."

She laughed. "Oh, I forget you have not been brought up in

"Follow us to the great house on the left"

Scotland," and stepping round him, she jerked the ring rapidly
up and down the corkscrew iron, making a loud ringing sound
that hummed and vibrated about the courtyard.

"What a wonderful thing!" James exclaimed. "May I have a
turn at it, Aunt Barbara?"

"We had better wait first and see if anyone comes."

They waited, but no one came, though they could hear voices
and laughter from inside, beyond the great door. Then,
through a top floor casement on their right, a head of shining
coppery curls was thrust. A girl almost of James's age laughed
down at them mischievously.

"You'll need to tirl mighty hard," she told them. "Old
Henry, the watchman, has slipped away for a quiet sleep by the
bakehouse fire and the rest of the folk are at their meat in the
big chamber, with the lassies serving them, and they'll not hear
you for the din of dishes."

"And why are you not at your meat too?" Barbara Ruthven
asked.

"Oh, I've been wicked again," the child told her. "I pulled
faces at my brother Alexander in the kirk yesterday during the
catechism and the minister caught me at it, and reproved me
before the whole congregation. And my grandmother said I
was to have no meat for a day, for bringing disgrace on the
family. It was really Alexander's fault, for if he hadn't cried
out like the ninny he is, the minister would never have noticed."

The girl seemed not in the least abashed, and her blue eyes
twinkled down at Barbara Ruthven, whose black eyes twinkled
back in return.

"And who is your grandmother, you naughty wee lass?"
Barbara asked her, her chuckle betraying her severe tone.

"Why, Lady Margaret Bruce, of course. My grandfather is
Sir George Bruce. I am Magdalen Bruce." Magdalen seemed
surprised at anyone not knowing who she was.

"Then we're kinsfolk. Why don't you come down and
welcome us?" James smiled up at her.

Magdalen leaned farther out of the window and smiled back.
"A kinsman, are you? I've never seen *you* before. Your name?"

"James Bruce. This is my aunt——" he began.

But Barbara Ruthven hastily broke in, "We will wait for
introductions further till we have spoken to Sir George Bruce,

James. But perhaps you could carry a message to your grand-father?" she asked Magdalen.

"Indeed, madam, I would if I could, but I am locked in this room. It is part of my punishment," she said without resentment. "I do not mind it, really. There is plenty to see along the shore and over the Firth with the boats coming and going. Only I'm getting right hungry," she added honestly.

James Bruce laughed outright. "I have some sweetmeats in my pocket," he said. "Can you catch?"

"Try me!"

He threw up a silk bag of comfits which she caught deftly. "Thank you, kinsman," she cried, her face dimpling into another laugh.

Barbara Ruthven tirled again at the pin a little impatiently. The two sailors had put down their wooden boxes at the top of the steps, and stood by them awkwardly, not knowing whether to go away or not. The position was rather ridiculous. Magdalen came to their rescue, however, with a suggestion.

"If I were you, I should send one of those men round to the bakehouse to seek old Henry. He had better tell him that important visitors have arrived in the ship. That will rouse Henry quickly enough. The bakehouse is round the corner to the left, at the end of the building."

One of the sailors who spoke English said, "I will go, madam," and set off round the building. In a moment or two he returned with old Henry wiping the sleep from his eyes and looking sheepish.

"Your pardon, madam. I did not know the master was expecting anyone off the Dutch ship. He said nothing to me of it. What message shall I give him?"

Magdalen leaned still farther out of the window. "Remember your manners, Henry. These are kinsfolk. Take them to the parlour to await my grandfather's coming," she instructed him.

"Get back, you wee beesom, you!" Henry said, with all the freedom of an old servant who has watched the children grow up, and their parents before them. He shook his fist at her. "You'll be falling out of that window, and you in disgrace too!" But he obeyed her directions and said to Lady Barbara, "Follow me, madam, if you please."

"And our boxes? What of them?" she asked.

Henry scratched his head, a little undecided what to do about these kinsfolk of his master's who seemed to have arrived without warning. Sir George was famed for his hospitality, however, and after all that wee rascal Magdalen had said they were kin.

"Those fellows had better bring the boxes to the parlour too," he decided. "My lady Bruce will say where they are to be carried later."

The little procession entered a door to the left at the top of a flight of stone steps and found themselves entering straight into the parlour. Barbara Ruthven paid the sailors for their trouble and Henry departed to tell his master of their arrival. In two high-backed oaken chairs they sat to await Sir George Bruce's pleasure, and Barbara's mind was clouded with misgivings about the way they might be received, and whether she had done right to return with James Bruce to Scotland. In the next room they could hear the clatter of pewter plates and tankards and the hum of voices and laughter, for Sir George Bruce sat at the head of the table with his family and servants, as was the fashion among the nobility in those days. There was a massive silver salt cellar on the table, and the family and guests sat above it, while servants and underlings occupied the places below. Suddenly Sir George banged with his fist on the table, there was a scraping of benches on the floor, a sudden silence, then Sir George's voice asking a blessing on the food which had been eaten. There was a loud "Amen!" then the sound of benches being replaced. Barbara Ruthven braced herself for the encounter that was to come.

Old Henry approached his master, who was talking earnestly with his son, another George Bruce, and waited patiently at his elbow till he noticed him.

"Well, Henry?"

"Sir, there are two of your kinsfolk waiting in the parlour to see you, a lady and a young lad. They have just come from the Dutch ship *Hans Pieter*."

Sir George wrinkled his brows. "I have no kinsfolk in Holland. Who can these be?" He turned to his son. "Come with me, George."

The two men, followed by Henry, came into the parlour from the Long Gallery where they dined. As soon as they entered,

"This is James Bruce who is indeed your kinsman"

James Bruce sprang to his feet and made a low bow to his kins-
men. Mistress Barbara curtsied in the manner she had learned
at the Scottish court. Sir George bowed too, but he lifted his
eyebrows questioningly. "Your pardon, madam, but you have
the advantage of me."

"You knew me well, George Bruce, when I was a young
lassie at the King's court. Maybe sorrow has changed me, but
there was a time when we footed it together with the best when
King James gave a ball at Falkland Palace."

Sir George Bruce stared harder at her, then gave an exclamation that had something of consternation in it. "The Lady
Barbara, by thunder! But why are you come here? The gate-
keeper said you were kinsfolk."

"In a way we are, through this boy here." She thrust James
Bruce gently forward. "This is James Bruce who is indeed your
kinsman, for you were uncle to his father, and you are therefore
great-uncle to him."

"Uncle to his father? But who is his father?" Sir George was
plainly mystified. "Henry, back to the door. This is no concern
of yours."

"My father was Edward Bruce, Lord Kinloss, sir," James
Bruce said, when the parlour door was shut.

Sir George's mouth fell open with astonishment. "But—but
Edward Bruce never married," he stammered.

"You are mistaken there, sir. Lord Kinloss did marry and I
was a witness to it," Barbara Ruthven told him.

"Whom did he marry?" Sir George asked sharply.

"My niece, Elizabeth."

"A Ruthven?" There was no doubt of the chagrin in Sir
George's voice.

"Yes, a Ruthven indeed." Barbara's voice was proudly cold.
"The child of my brother, the Earl of Gowrie, by a secret
marriage when he was a youth in Italy."

The hot blood mounted into Sir George's face. "Gowrie's
child!" he exclaimed.

"Sit down, sir," the younger George Bruce urged his father
with some concern. He placed a chair for Lady Barbara too.
"Pray be seated, madam. This business might take some sorting
out. May I ask when and where my Cousin Kinloss was
married?"

"In Paris, more than twelve years ago," she told him.

"Were there other witnesses to the marriage?"

"There was one, Nan Cranston, who had been my nurse. Lord Kinloss and Elizabeth Ruthven were hand-fasted in the Scottish custom before us and declared that they took each other for man and wife."

George Bruce was quick to pounce upon a word. "You say there *was* a witness. Where is she now?"

"She was an old woman even then and died during our journeyings. We have lived in many lands, the boy and I, and I brought him up after he lost both father and mother."

"So you are the only witness to the marriage?" Sir George asked abruptly.

"Yes." She gave an unhappy sigh. "I know that I am a Ruthven but my word is none the less to be believed for that."

Sir George looked uncomfortable and he and his son exchanged glances.

"Madam, I do not cast doubt upon your word, but why have you delayed so long in bringing this lad to Scotland?"

"Need you ask that?" she retorted bitterly. "Would his life have been safe if King James had known of him? You know what he swore to do to the Ruthvens. Lately I have heard that the King is not quite so bitter against my brother whom he imprisoned in the Tower, and that emboldened me to bring James Bruce to his home at last."

Sir George shook his head and passed his hand thoughtfully over his short pointed beard. "But why have you come to *me*? Why did you not go to Thomas, Edward Kinloss's own brother, who fell heir to his estates at his death?"

"Do you think he would place this child's interests before his own? Would he be likely to want to give up his estate to the boy?" Barbara asked. "I came to you, Sir George Bruce, because you have always had the reputation of being a just, honest man. Edward Bruce thought well of you, and at his death he sent a message to his wife Elizabeth to bring his son to you, and you would see that right was done by him; but she did not outlive him by many days."

Sir George's grim expression softened, but he looked troubled. "I doubt how this lad's claim to his father's estate would stand in a court of law, my lady. You are the only witness left of the marriage. You have no writing to prove that the marriage took place, have you?"

Barbara shook her head unhappily. "It was a secret marriage, and Kinloss always hoped to celebrate a public one in England before the King."

"It is a pity that you have no writing then to prove that this lad is indeed Kinloss's son, and to show the Council in Edinburgh. What I mean, madam, is that though your word is good enough for me, it might not be enough for the law courts."

Barbara, in her turn, began to look worried. James looked in bewilderment from one to the other. Then George Bruce the younger put in a question. "You say Kinloss's marriage took place Scots fashion in Paris? Would such a marriage be recognized under French law? And if it is not legal in France, would the Scots lawyers regard it as legal either? The point is sure to be made."

His father nodded agreement. "There would be many difficulties in making a claim to the Kinloss estates now, and I doubt if the King would favour the cause of one who is half a Ruthven, madam." Sir George spoke plainly. "It would put me in an awkward situation both with Thomas, the present Lord Kinloss, who is my neighbour and relation too, and also with the King, whose favour I have the honour to enjoy."

Barbara Ruthven's eyes flashed. "If you value the King's favour more than your duty to this lad's father, I have no more to say to you. I had hoped you would have done something for the boy, for the sake of the love you once bore his father, and—and—a little for the sake of the old days when we were both young at Falkland. We will not trouble you further, sir. We will go—we will go——" Her voice faltered and broke.

"Where shall we go, Aunt Barbara? You said we had little money," the boy reminded her innocently.

"I—I—doubtless I can find friends in Perth." She held up her head proudly.

"What shall we do then about the casket?" James Bruce asked. "Will Sir George see it is placed in the Abbey of Culross as my father wished?"

"What casket is this?" Sir George demanded.

For answer Barbara Ruthven knelt beside one of the boxes, lifted the lid, and brought out the small silver casket.

"It holds the heart of Edward Bruce, Lord Kinloss. It was his wish that it should be buried in the Abbey Church of Culross that he loved." The tears welled up into her eyes. "As we can stay here no longer, will you do this?"

Sir George's generous heart could not withstand her tears.

"It is the boy's right and duty to carry out his father's wish," he said. "Will you not stay a short while here, madam, so that it can be done?"

"I thank you, sir. If you are not afraid it will put you out of the King's favour, then we will stay." Her lip curled a little.

"Are we to stay, Aunt Barbara? Are we to stay?" the boy asked in some excitement.

"For a short time."

He turned eagerly to Sir George Bruce. "Then, please, sir, if it be possible, could I—would you permit me to go down your coal-mine that goes under the sea? I saw it from the ship, and the captain of the *Hans Pieter* told me of its wonders. He pointed out to me, too, the great Egyptian wheel that you have constructed to pump the water out of the mine. Would you let me see it working? I—I have a great fancy to see these things, but if it would be too much trouble——" The boy's voice faltered into silence.

Sir George was looking at him with quickened interest. "Why, lad, if you have a care for these matters, then you are a bairn after my own heart." He clapped him on the shoulder. "My faith, but you *shall* stay! After all, you are my kinsman, and Edward Bruce's son. I mind well how he took a lively interest in my mine too."

"Thank you, sir. And my Aunt Barbara? May she stay too, for I owe her very much indeed?"

Sir George smiled over the boy's head at Lady Barbara, a kind generous smile. "If you will, Mistress Barbara? And not just for the sake of the bairn, but for the memory of those old days at Falkland."

She dropped him a curtsy. "Thank you, Sir George. Yes, I will stay."

Sir George's business caution returned to him. "I shall be pleased to have you both for my guests, but, for the sake of the boy, it might be as well if no one knows who he is, or who you are too, for the matter of that, till the way seems clearer for his affairs. We shall say that you are distant kinsfolk, if that will satisfy you?"

"I must be content. With little money and no home, there is nothing else for us to do," Barbara Ruthven said with blunt honesty.

"Then I will speak with my wife and arrange for you to be housed. Your pardon if I leave you for a few minutes."

His son looked a little awkwardly at Barbara Ruthven. "You have been living in Holland, madam?" he asked politely.

"For a short time, yes."

"You would learn to speak Dutch, then?" George Bruce turned to the boy.

"Yes, sir, a little, but not so well as my Aunt Barbara speaks it. I speak Italian better."

"Oh, so you speak Italian?" George Bruce looked at him with interest. James began to reply, but Barbara Ruthven interrupted him quickly.

"The boy has had some schooling in Italy." She frowned a little at James, and a silence fell among them which might have been awkward but for the hasty arrival of a lad about the same age as James.

"Father, I helped Andrew Brown to repair the gear on the Egyptian wheel. It's working fine now——" He broke off in some confusion. "Your pardon, sir! I did not know you were entertaining visitors." He would have gone out again but his father placed a hand on his shoulder.

"Wait, lad," he said kindly. "Here is a distant cousin of yours, James Bruce, come to visit us from over the North Sea, along with his aunt, the Lady Barbara." Barbara Ruthven noticed that he did not mention her surname. "This is my son, Edward Bruce," he told them.

Edward bowed low over Barbara's hand, then turned to James. For a moment the two boys stood looking at each other, the golden fairness of Edward Bruce contrasted with the dark eyes and hair of James. Then James's frank smile was reflected in the warmth of Edward's. "You are welcome, indeed, Cousin," he said, giving a slightly old-fashioned bow and putting out his hand to James. James grasped it firmly. Between the two of them ran the spark of sudden warm friendship.

"Thank you, Cousin Edward. Did you say you had been mending the big Egyptian wheel?" James asked.

"Yes, the cogs on the big vertical wheel were not quite matching the cogs on the horizontal wheel. I found out the reason, Father, before Andrew Brown did," Edward Bruce told George proudly.

"Had one of the pillars supporting the horizontal wheel sunk a little?" James asked.

Edward stared at him open-mouthed. "It had, but how did *you* know?"

"I just guessed, partly from what I saw of the machinery from the ship, and partly from what I have learned in mathematics."

Edward looked at him with respect. "I, too, am studying mathematics, but I do not get on very fast with them, for the minister, Mr. Colville, who teaches me is more interested in the Latin."

George Bruce smiled a little. He had sympathy with his son's preference for mathematics. "Maybe you and James could help each other in your studies."

"Why? Will James be staying here?" Edward asked eagerly.

"For a while, perhaps."

"I hope it will be long enough to let Edward show me the big Egyptian wheel and the underwater coal-mine," James said.

"I think we can promise that," George Bruce laughed.

"Could we go find Andrew Brown *now*? He would show James the workings of the mine." Edward was no less eager than James.

"Not just now. Your grandfather has gone to fetch your grandmother to meet our visitors, so James must stay here," his father told him.

The faces of both boys fell, so openly that Lady Barbara was driven to laughter. "Was there ever a Bruce who was not mad about machinery?"

"True! We Bruces have a fondness for seeing wheels turn," he laughed back at her.

It was on their laughter that Lady Bruce swept with great dignity into the room. Barbara Ruthven rose at once and curtsied low, and James made his most courtier-like bow, clicking his heels together in the continental fashion. Lady Bruce acknowledged their greetings graciously, but she did not smile and she did not extend her hand.

"So you have come back to Scotland, Lady Barbara?" she said, but there was no hint of welcome in her voice.

"A long overdue return, my lady," Barbara Ruthven replied, and they exchanged long cool looks. "I have not come altogether on my own account," she added, nodding towards James.

"So I understand. Well, in the name of kinship we must see you well lodged." Though the words were fair enough there was little warmth in them, and the colour mounted in Lady Barbara's face. "Have old Henry take these boxes to the new lodging, into the east room on the top floor," Lady Bruce said to her son. She turned again to Lady Barbara. "There is a small room off the larger room where your nephew James Bruce can sleep."

"Thank you, Lady Margaret."

"It will serve till some other lodging can be found for you in the town," Lady Margaret went on. "As you no doubt know, we are a big family, with children and grandchildren. We have not the accommodation for guests to stay with us for a long while, for my husband has many visitors to see him in connection with his business ventures, but he will see that you are *fittingly* housed." There was a little sneering stress on the word "fittingly" that showed Lady Bruce regarded their visitors in the light of embarrassing poor relations.

Hot anger flooded Barbara Ruthven's face. Sir George hastily said, "I am sorry we have already dined, but some refreshment will be served to you in your rooms while you unpack your boxes. Perhaps you will join us at supper later on?"

"Thank you, Sir George," Lady Barbara said, with a meekness that had a hint of mockery in it. "Perhaps I might be shown my chamber?"

"I will send for a serving woman——" Lady Bruce was beginning, in a voice intended to show that she herself had no intention of leading the way, when a younger woman who had come quietly into the room stepped forward with impetuous kindness.

"If you'll allow me, my lady, I'll conduct our visitor to her room."

Lady Bruce frowned. "If it pleases you, Mary," she said coldly. "This is my son's wife, Mary Preston of Valleyfield." She was forced to make the introduction. "Our guest is Lady Barbara Ruthven." There was a momentary shocked silence in the room.

It was broken by Sir George. "I think we decided it might be wiser for all of us if Lady Barbara's second name were not mentioned publicly." He gave Lady Bruce a reproving look. "I shall be obliged, Lady Barbara, if you will take some other name for your own sake, as well as mine, while you are at Culross."

"Then, as I am to be under your protection, sir, and because my nephew's name is the same as yours, may I take the name of Bruce too?" Lady Barbara asked. "It is a name I might well have borne, if fate had not taken me from Scotland when I was so young." She smiled mockingly at Lady Bruce.

Her meaning was quite plain to Sir George and his wife, and it was Lady Bruce's turn to flush with anger, but she could only pretend not to understand. Barbara Ruthven had scored the last word, and sweeping a triumphant curtsy she left the room in the wake of Mary Preston, the younger George Bruce's wife.

When the family reassembled for supper that night in the Long Gallery with its beautiful green-panelled walls and the long oak tables set with shining pewter plates and tankards, James found himself placed next to Edward among the Bruce children and he was very content. Not so content was Barbara Ruthven! Lady Bruce had taken a puny revenge upon her by placing her well down the table instead of in the guest's place of honour on Sir George's right hand. She excused herself with a mocking smile. "Seeing you have joined our family, Mistress Bruce, it will be as well to allot you a place within the family, rather than as a guest. Perhaps you will take the seat below my son's wife, Mary Preston, and next to the children. Mary prefers to sit near her children, as they are somewhat unruly."

Pride would not let Barbara Ruthven show the hurt to her feelings and she took her place with quiet dignity. Once Sir George had said grace and the clatter of the plates had begun, Mary Preston took the opportunity to whisper to Barbara, "I am glad you are sitting next to me, Mistress Barbara, although you should have been given the place of honour."

Barbara shrugged her shoulders. "My family has had to suffer worse blows. But I like your 'somewhat unruly' brood. They look fine healthy bairns."

Mary looked pleased at the compliment. "Edward and James seem to have become great friends. I am glad."

Barbara looked at the children and knitted her brows. She missed one face among them. "Are all your children here?" she asked.

"All but the baby who is with her nurse, and—and Magdalen who is in disgrace for misbehaving in church. My mother-in-law ordered that she should keep her chamber and have no food."

Barbara Ruthven's eyes widened. "Does your mother-in-law deal out punishment to *your* children, then?"

Mary looked rebellious for a moment. "You have seen how it is with her. She must always be first and order things, or there is no peace, and I am a stupid weak body who gives in for the sake of peace, though I think Magdalen has been punished enough for what was a childish piece of nonsense."

"So do I!" Barbara agreed heartily. "Why do you not say she must come to the table with the others?"

"Do you think I dare?" Mary asked dubiously.

"Why not? She is *your* child."

"Why then, so I will," Mary declared.

There happened one of those pauses when everyone is suddenly silent. Mary seized her chance and with heightened colour she cleared her throat and addressed her mother-in-law. "My lady, I ask that Magdalen be pardoned and come to the table with the other children to meet her Cousin James."

Lady Bruce frowned and pursed her lips. "She has been a naughty child and deserves punishment," she began.

"She has had enough punishment, I think." For once Mary Preston glowered back at her mother-in-law in defiance, a thing which had never happened before to Margaret Bruce.

George Bruce looked from his wife to his mother and back again. It was plain that in spite of Mary's determination she was near to tears, and that she had been goaded enough. George spoke quietly but firmly, "Mother, it is my wish that Magdalen should take her place with the other children too."

The children's chatter died down; there was silence among

the older people as everyone looked to Lady Margaret Bruce. She knew that she was faced with an open rebellion in her own family, and she did not wish to lose face before Barbara Ruthven. She fell back on a dignified withdrawal, masking it by an air of graciousness, making it seem that her permission had been asked by George Bruce.

"Very well, George, as you ask it. The child may come to the table." She turned to one of the serving maids, "Bessie, go bring Mistress Magdalen from her room. Here is the key." She detached the key from a bunch she carried on a chain at her waist. Then she turned her attention again to her plate as though a trifling incident had been closed.

Presently Bessie returned with Magdalen. The child entered the room with head held high. With a coolness that matched Lady Bruce's own, she paused by her grandmother's chair and gave her a level stare for the cold glance she received. Then she swept a low curtsy that had more than a hint of mockery in it.

"Are you sorry for your naughty conduct in church, bringing disgrace on the whole family?" her grandmother asked. The child did not answer, but again she swept a deep curtsy that might mean agreement, though her bright blue eyes remained defiant. Lady Bruce thought it better to assume that the girl was penitent. "Very well. You may go to your place," she said.

With a toss of her tawny red curls, Magdalen took her seat next to her brother Edward. A maidservant brought her a plate of meat and was about to set it before her when Lady Bruce rapped out, "I have not said you can serve meat to Mistress Magdalen. That part of her punishment must stand. She must go hungry. She has a proud spirit that needs subduing."

Mary Preston looked indignantly at her, and George half rose from his chair to protest, when Sir George looked up from his plate. "Och, the child has been punished! Leave it at that, wife." But Magdalen herself waved the servant away.

"I would rather not eat, thank you, Bessie. To go hungry is good for the flesh as well as the spirit." Though it was said with apparent meekness, Magdalen darted a saucy glance at her grandmother's more than plump form, then folded her hands demurely on the table and bent her head. There was nothing Lady Bruce could say, and Sir George called out sharply, "You children get on with your meat."

From under her brows Magdalen winked at Edward and then at James. James saw Edward sneak a piece of meat and oatcake into his pocket under cover of the linen cloth and he did the same. Magdalen gave a sly little chuckle. "Try to hide a piece of cheese too for me, James, please."

"And a rosy-cheeked apple?" James asked her out of the corner of his mouth.

"If you can manage it, yes."

When the children left the table and made their bows and curtsies to Sir George and Lady Bruce, Magdalen wore a smug little air of triumph.

"Your pockets, child?" Lady Bruce said in sudden suspicion.

Demurely Magdalen turned out her pockets, empty save for a handkerchief, made a bobbing curtsy again, then ran to catch up with James and Edward as they crossed the forecourt to the other house.

CHAPTER 3

THE MINE

THAT night James leaned through his casement window and looked at the moon rising across the Forth. Below him on the dark shore there glowed the light of fifty fires, the sparks flying upwards from them. Against the leaping flames he could see the outlines of figures bending over the great iron cauldrons supported on stones built like narrow walls on each side of the fires. Edward Bruce leaned beside him.

"My aunt said those people were making salt," James said.

"Yes. They drive off the water as steam and the salt is left behind in the great pans."

"There are women and children there too?"

"Oh, yes, whole families work together at the salt pans. It is not hard to do, but the fires have to be kept going day and night."

"What do they do with the salt?" James asked.

Edward looked surprised at the question. "Why, they make it for my grandfather, of course. All the foreshore belongs to him. He pays them so much a cauldron for the salt they make. Sometimes they make as much as a hundred tons in a week," he added proudly.

James's eyes grew big. "Whatever does Sir George do with all that salt?"

"He sells it to the merchants, of course. It is used for salting herring and beef and mutton. King James has given my grandfather the sole right to supply some English towns with salt, King's Lynn and Boston and Hull. Our ships sail there every week, as well as to Holland and Flanders. They carry Culross girdles, too, as well as salt."

"What on earth is a Culross girdle?" James asked.

Edward chuckled at his cousin's ignorance. "It's a kind of flat pan without sides. The womenfolk bake scones and oat-cakes on them. We sell a lot of them to Holland."

"I had no idea there was so much trade from Culross."

"Oh, aye! That is how the Bruces made their fortune, from salt and coal. My grandfather is a great man of business, and so is my father," Edward told him. "My grandfather invented the machinery too, to drain the coal-pit under the Forth."

"Will you show me that tomorrow, please?"

"Indeed I will."

"What do you want to do when you are grown up, Edward?"

"Invent machines to mine coal better," Edward said promptly. "What are *you* going to do, James?"

James bit his lip. "I don't rightly know, Edward. My aunt Barbara says I have a right to lands about here that belong to Lord Kinloss."

Edward eyed him narrowly. "You mean the great house at the top of the hill, the Abbey House, they call it? You will not find it easy to claim from Lord Kinloss. He is a kinsman of ours."

"My Aunt Barbara knows more about it than I do. She brought me up after I was left an orphan, so I would do anything to please her, but for my part, I would rather be a doctor."

"A *doctor*?" Edward looked astonished.

"Yes; my uncle, Patrick Ruthven, is a doctor. All the nineteen years the King kept him a prisoner in the Tower of London he studied medicine till he was able to take his place as a doctor. It is a wonderful thing, to be able to heal the sick. All the Ruthvens are skilled in medicine, even my Aunt Barbara."

"Is she?" Edward asked in surprise.

James bit his lip. "Perhaps I should not have mentioned that. She does not like it talked about."

"Why not? Is it because medicine is near witchcraft and the Black Arts?"

"What makes you say that?" James asked quickly.

"A thing I overheard my grandmother say to my grandfather. She did not know I was close by. She said, 'All the Ruthvens are dabblers in witchcraft and the Black Arts. Are you going to let that woman stay here to poison us all?' she asked."

James's eyes blazed. "Poison? My aunt would not poison anyone!"

"Och! Take no notice of it. My grandmother is aye getting a bee in her bonnet about this or that," Edward laughed.

James still looked angry. "Your grandfather might believe it."

"Not he! He lets my grandmother have her way in the house, more's the pity, but he follows his own mind in other matters. You have nothing to fear."

All the same, James looked troubled and his brow did not clear till Edward said, "Tomorrow we will get up early and go down the mine when the night-shift comes off work and the day-shift goes down."

"Do the miners work night and day too?" James asked.

"Oh, yes! As it is dark down the mine and they have to work by the light of lanterns, it is as easy to work by night as by day. But we are not miners, so we'd better get our sleep. Be ready early in the morning."

The next morning the two boys stole down the stone stairs at the first light, across the courtyard to the Sand Haven before the family was up. The watchman nodded in his chair by the door and gave them a sleepy "Good day!" Edward turned to the right and went about a quarter of a mile westward along the road that wound by the shore. A clattering noise of machinery grew louder, and, as they rounded a bend in the road, they came suddenly on Sir George Bruce's Egyptian wheel.

"There!" Edward exclaimed, full of pride. "My grandfather designed that."

Three sturdy horses were yoked to a beam coming from a big horizontal wheel. Round and round they went in a never-ending circle, urged on occasionally when they flagged by a flick from a whip wielded by their driver. An overseer was watching the working of the machinery with a critical eye. He was a tall, broadly built man about thirty-five years old, with a tanned skin that bore the occasional blue flecks that come from working among coal for many years.

"Well, Andrew, I've brought my Cousin James Bruce to see our wheel," Edward told the overseer. "Will you explain to him how it works, please?"

Andrew replied, "Aye, aye, I'll tell him," in a quiet serious manner. "You see this big wheel the horses are birling round? And you see the other big upright wheel on yon beam overhead? Weel, the two o' them have cogs that fit into each other, and when the horizontal wheel is pulled round by the horses, it pushes the other wheel too. Yon overhead wheel is fastened to a shaft which it turns, and if you look at the end of it there, you'll see a chain with buckets fastened on to it. Yon upright wheel hauls the buckets out of the mine. There are thirty-six buckets. Eighteen are going up, while eighteen are going down, in an endless chain."

"The buckets are tipping water into a trough, aren't they?" James asked.

"Aye. They've scooped the water up out o' a kind o' drain in the mine, carried it up and emptied it into yon trench and the water runs back into the sea."

"That's a very clever invention," James remarked. "Is the mine very wet, then?"

"Weel, there's a deal o' water seeps in, but nothing the buckets can't deal with. Whiles there's a high tide wi' a following wind, and we get a drop more water than ordinar' in the mine, but it's no' bad."

"Do you think we can go down the mine this morning?" Edward asked.

Andrew Brown hesitated. "The last time I took ye down the mine her ladyship was no' so pleased wi' me. She said you got your doublet all clarty wi' the muck o' the pit."

"It is all right this time, Andrew. Both my grandfather and my father have said I can show James the coal-mine. That is one of the reasons he is staying with us, so he can see it."

"Ah, weel, then, if your grandfather is willing." Andrew was quite pleased to give in to Edward's persuasive tongue. He had been at the making of the coal-pit and seen the Egyptian wheel devised and erected, and he was as proud of the underwater mine as his master. He led the way towards the mine entrance near the shore. A stone hut was built over the pit shaft. From a niche in the wall he took three lanterns fitted with candles, and with flint and tinder he lighted each one. As he did it, he talked to James. "Ye know this is the only mine in the world that goes under the sea?"

"So I understand, sir," James replied politely.

"Ye can call me Andrew as the other bairns do. This mine, ye might say, then, is one o' the nine wonders o' the world." Andrew's voice swelled with pride.

"How far does it go down under the Firth of Forth?" James asked.

"More than a mile, my laddie. When men are at work under-
neath, a hundred of the greatest ships in Britain could sail over
their heads."

James let out a whistle of astonishment that pleased Andrew
Brown greatly. "How did men manage to dig it out under the
sea?"

"You know how the coal lies in seams in the ground?"

James looked a little puzzled. "I have never been down a
coal-mine before."

"You know how the veins run in a man's body?"

"Yes."

"Weel, ye might say the coal runs in veins through the earth.
This coal we mine under the sea is a thick vein of very good
coal. Sir George found it first by digging on the land, and he
found the seam of coal ran under the Firth, and he determined
to get it. But come with me and I'll show you how he did it.
Take your lantern and watch where you put your feet, for some
of the ladders down into the mine are right slippery."

He led them forward to a low stone coping around what
seemed to be a well. "This is the first shaft," Andrew said, and
by the light of his lantern James saw the rungs of a ladder disappearing into the darkness below. At the foot of the ladder
another lantern twinkled twenty feet down.

"I'll go first, then you, James, and Edward will follow. There
is a knotted rope runs down by the ladder that you can grasp
to steady yourself. When you reach the foot of the ladder stand
still beside me till your eyes grow more accustomed to the
darkness." Andrew swung himself with accustomed ease over
the stone coping.

James put his lantern down on top of the stone wall while he
took the top rungs of the ladder in his hands and climbed over
rather gingerly on to it. He reached up again for the lantern
and Edward put it into his hand. "Take care you don't drop it or
you might hit Andrew on the head with it," he warned James.

"Aye, take care o' that," Andrew added. "I've no wish to be
knocked out and finish up in the sump at the bottom of the
mine. Maybe it would be better if you just gave me your lantern
too, James, and that leaves you both hands free to hang on to
the ladder. Just feel with your feet for the rungs. Take your
time now."

Andrew took the two lanterns in his great fist and shone them so that they cast a pool of light about James's feet. Slowly, rung by rung, James followed him, and it was with a sigh of relief that he found himself standing alongside Andrew.

"Stop and catch your breath, laddie, before we go any farther down."

"Why, aren't we at the bottom?" James asked in surprise.

"Jings, no! There are two more ladders yet."

James found he was standing on a kind of platform of rock from which yet another ladder descended to the depths below. All around him was the din and clank of machinery. By the light of his lantern Edward saw his cousin's puzzled look.

"Those are the buckets on the endless chain draining the water out of the pit. They go up another shaft alongside us here," he shouted in James's ear. On his other side Andrew took hold of his arm and gave him instructions in his other ear.

"We'll wait here a minute to give those below time to come up. There are some on the ladder now."

James peered down the shaft. There were twinkling points of light at the foot of it and on the ladder itself three strange figures seemed to be ascending. He held up his own lantern to see better when the first one reached the top. He gave a gasp of astonishment. What he had taken to be a hunchback was a girl about his own age carrying a wicker creel on her back, full of coal. She was followed by a boy even younger, then by a woman. All three wore tattered dirty clothing; their feet were bare and their faces were black with coal dust, so that they looked like strange demons of the underworld.

"Do children work in the mines too?" James asked in surprise.

"Why, yes!" Andrew Brown seemed even more surprised at the question. "The men hew the coal; the little bairns fill the baskets and bags wi' the coal, and the women and bigger bairns carry it out o' the mines."

"Are there still smaller children working down there in the darkness?" James's voice was pitying.

"Oh, aye. The miner's bairns work alongside their father as soon as they can learn to fill a basket. It takes every pair of hands to earn bread to feed so many mouths."

"And do the other children go up and down the ladders all day? Don't they get tired?"

What he had taken to be a hunchback was a girl about his own age carrying a wicker creel on her back

"Aye, at first they do, but after a while their legs and backs get used to it."

"Do they ever slip and fall from the ladders?" James asked.

"Whiles they do if they're careless, but the chance of a broken neck or a broken limb soon teaches them care. They get sure-footed, like cats, very soon."

"Poor children! It must be terrible to work in the darkness all the time." James spoke his thought aloud.

"Och, they get used to it, and someone has to win the coal from the earth. There are bound to be accidents in every mine. I dinna think we get more than ordinar' in this one. Sir George is particular about the ladders being in good order and plenty o' lanterns at the foot and top."

"If you bring up the water in buckets, why could you not bring up the coal that way?" James asked.

Through the gloom Andrew and Edward stared at him.

"My sakes, laddie, but it would cost a mint o' money to rig another wheel to take coal buckets up and down. And they'd still need filling," Andrew told him.

"All the same, James has got a good notion there," Edward gave his opinion. "Maybe some day *I'll* invent a kind of machine to carry up the coal."

"And what would the poor miners' families do then for a living? You young ones are all alike. You'd alter the world to suit your own notions," Andrew laughed. "But come along down the other ladders now."

The two boys followed him to the foot of the mine. The last ladder ended at the entrance to a long tunnel in which James was surprised to find that he could stand upright.

"I always heard people had to crawl along the tunnels in coal-mines," he remarked.

"Aye, in many other mines they do, but this is the best of mines," Andrew told him. "In most places in it a man can walk upright, except at the parts where the miners are hewing away at the coal. Come and see."

He led the way along a narrower passage that branched off from the tunnel. As they went along they met women and girls walking along with baskets of coal on their backs and they stood sideways to let Andrew and the boys pass. At last they came to a small cave hewn in the black shining coal. In it, on their knees, for they could not stand upright, two grimy miners, wearing only tattered breeches, swung away with their pick-axes at the wall of coal. As it fell away in black lumps, a lad shovelled it from round them. Four dirty urchins, like black imps, with smaller shovels loaded it into wicker baskets and stacked them at the entrance for the women and bigger girls to carry up to the light of day. A big lad helped to load the baskets on to the backs of the women, as if they were beasts of burden. A flat leather band passed round their foreheads like a cap, then like a sling round the bottom of the basket. This took part of the weight of the basket and left the women's hands free to climb the ladders, and for one hand to support the weight of the basket behind the woman. Then, bent almost double, the women made their way along the tunnel and up the ladder.

A dark-haired, black-eyed girl was standing defiantly in a corner, her mother scolding furiously at her.

"What's the matter, Ann?" Andrew asked the woman.

"It's this lazy good-for-nothing lass. She doesna' want to carry the coal. I tell her, 'No coal, no bread!' She'll go without food when the day's turn is finished."

The tears rolled down the girl's face, making two rivulets through the coal dust.

"What's wrong wi' you, lassie?" Andrew asked sternly.

"It's my back, mister. It's that sore. I canna bear the weight o' the coal on it," the girl sobbed.

"Och, ye'll get used to it," her mother told her roughly. "I had to start the carrying afore I was twelve years old, and so must you. Lift her basket, Tom," she directed the lad.

The girl set her teeth and grimaced with pain as the basket was lifted to her back, but she dared not disobey. Staggering slightly she set off for the foot of the ladders. Andrew noticed the look of concern on James's face.

"It aye gails their backs a bit at the beginning but soon their skins get hardened and used to the load," he told James. James shook his head in pity, but he made no reply. "Come and see the other part of the mine now," Andrew invited him. "You'll see something right marvellous, I promise."

As they made their way back to the main tunnel James felt a cold current of fresh air blowing into his face. "There's quite a wind," he said in surprise.

"You're down under the waters of the Forth now," Andrew announced impressively. "You'll feel a draught, though, because this mine has two entrances to it."

The tinkling sound of water grew. All around them the arched walls ran with moisture which dripped into little runnels hewn out of the rock. The water was carried by them into a deeper trough which ran along one side of the tunnel.

"It's wetter now than usual because the tide's up," Andrew explained. "The water that seeps through is carried by yon trough to the sump at the foot of the shaft. From there it's hoisted up by the bucket chain you saw. Aye, Sir George planned it all, drainage and machinery too."

James noticed that they passed several bearers of coal moving in the same direction as themselves, which seemed to be yet farther under the waters of the Forth and away from the main shaft. "Aren't they going the wrong way?" he asked.

"Wait and see, laddie," Andrew chuckled.

On each side of the tunnel a maze of small passages led towards the coal seams. At the entrance to each one a guttering candle flamed in a lantern.

"Sir George aye keeps the mine well lighted," Andrew said proudly. "There are some mine-owners grudge the price o' candles, but no' Sir George. And this is the only mine in Scotland where ye can walk upright."

Soon they found themselves in the wake of a procession of bearers carrying their loads. At a widening of the tunnel the women stood aside respectfully to let them pass. Among them James noticed the gipsy-like girl, her face tense and her lips pressed closely together. A lantern set in the wall at the foot of the shaft threw its beam on James's face and she could not help seeing the look of compassion he gave her. For a moment the misery of her young face lightened before the mask of suffering descended again. They reached the foot of the shaft. Far above them showed a circle of dim grey sky. Down the shaft a rhythmic roaring sound came to them.

"What's that noise?" James asked, puzzled.

"Wait till you poke your head into the daylight again, my lad, then you'll see."

The two boys followed Andrew up the ladders. This time it did not seem so difficult to James as the going down had been.

The circle of daylight up above him lent him confidence. At last they emerged into the full light of day.

James blinked hard and stared about him. He was on a circular platform of stone in the centre of which was the shaft. Round the platform a tremendously thick high wall was built. Steps were cut in the stonework and Andrew beckoned him to follow up them. The roaring sound grew louder still. James gave a cry of surprise when he saw the waves.

"Why, we're right out in the Firth of Forth on a tiny island!"

"Aye, but it wasna' always an island. Sir George built it. Fine he knew the coal-seams went under the water and this is the way he made to get at them."

"How could he do that?" James was puzzled.

"Weel, laddie, when the tide goes out, there are long banks of rock and sand. This island is built on one o' the reefs. Every time the tide went out, Sir George carted loads o' rock and clay on to the bank till it was built into a great mound. Then the men built a great thick wall round it."

"To keep the sea out?"

"Aye, and so it does, as you see. No matter how high the tide comes, it doesna' o'er-top this big wall."

James looked around him. Except for the blown spray off the top of the waves, no seawater slopped over the wall.

"After that was done, the master began to sink a shaft to look for the coal. The miners dug forty feet down through the rock. At last they came on what they expected—the sea coal, and they dug the mine forward into it."

"So that's how the mine came to have two entrances?" James commented.

"Aye, that's the way o' it. You might say it has two exits, as well, and a mighty useful one this is. Look down there below the wall."

A sailing boat with a deep hull was moored to iron rings in the wall. Already the hold was well filled with coal. A flight of wide steps descended from the top of the wall to it.

"This is where we load the coal," Andrew went on. "There's a channel dug round the wall and out to deep water in the Forth. The sea keeps these channels filled so we can load the boats whether the tide be high or low. That's why it's called 'The Moat Pit', for the boats can always float in the channel, even at low tide."

"Is that ship waiting to be loaded now?" James asked.

"Yes. The bearers go down those steps and tip their coal into the hold of the ship."

Even as he spoke, the line of bearers arrived on the platform of the moat. The overseer and the boys moved along the wall to give them room to descend the steps, and Andrew Brown kept an eye on the loading of the boat, but James turned to watch the bearers with their loads. Little did he know that this simple action was to change all his life!

The gipsy girl was in the middle of the line approaching the steps to mount the top of the wall. She was just in front of a lad about fifteen who threw taunts at her over her shoulder.

"Can you no' move any faster?" he jeered. "You snivellin' gipsy! Move out o' the way and let me up the steps afore ye. Ye've held me back long enough, crawling up yon ladders." He made as if to push her roughly aside as they came to the steps up to the moat wall, but the gipsy girl stood her ground, her eyes flashing dangerously.

"Keep your place behind me, John Horne," she cried, and barred his way with her out-thrust arm. He tried to push past her, but she was already on the steps. John Horne lost his temper and seized hold of her basket, pulling at it so that the band from it to her forehead jerked her head backwards. She lost her balance and fell from the steps to the stone platform, upsetting her creel of coal. The lad gave a jeering laugh and sped up the steps. At the top he found his way barred by a wrathful James.

"Down with you! Down with you at once and on your knees to help the lass to pick up her coal, you cowardly bully!" James Bruce commanded.

John Horne tried to brazen it out. "Och! She got in my way. She did it on purpose."

"I saw all that happened. Down with you at once!"

"Who are you to be ordering me?" Horne asked impudently. "I'll not go down."

"Oh, yes, you will! In the same way the girl did!" James Bruce leaped towards him. The lad thought James was going to strike him and dodged, but James was not aiming a blow at the lad. He seized the creel from Horne's back and flung it on to the paved platform below, scattering the coal, and pushed Horne after it.

"Now go down on your hands and knees and pick *your* coal up, if you will not help her with hers."

Andrew Brown and Edward Bruce had been so intent on watching the loading of the coal boat that they had not noticed what had happened. They sprang round at James's angry shout, saw Horne sprawling amid his coal and cursing angrily. James ran down the steps to the gipsy girl and began to help her to pile her coal in the creel again.

"No, no, young sir!" she begged him. "You'll get your bonnie clothes spoilt wi' the coal dust. It's no' for a young gentleman to be doing the likes o' that."

"What are you doing, James?" Andrew Brown asked, looking vexed. "What's going on down there?"

"That impudent lad thought he had the right to push a lass off the steps, so I just showed him what I thought of it," James said coolly.

"Och, lad, it would be better if ye didna interfere in the fights between the young folk in the mine. They can settle their own disputes." Andrew Brown bit his lip in annoyance. He raised his voice to the two bearers. "Get on wi' picking up yon coal, or I'll tak' a whip to both your backs."

James continued to pile coal into the girl's creel. Suddenly he saw blood running down her arm from a deep cut.

"You've hurt yourself!" he exclaimed.

"I caught my elbow against the edge of a stone when I fell. 'Tis naught."

"But your arm is black with coal dust. If it gets into that cut, it might take bad ways." James dropped his voice. "Listen to me. If you have any trouble with your arm—or the sore place on your back, come to see my aunt. She has great skill in healing and she will not turn you away. We are staying at Sir George Bruce's house. You must ask for Mistress Barbara Bruce. I will tell her about you."

Andrew Brown called down to him, "Come along, young sir. There's a boat waiting to take us back to the land."

"I must go now, but remember!" James told the girl. She nodded and her eyes misted over with sudden warm tears at the kindness in his voice. As James went up the wall steps John Horne scowled after him.

"I'll be quits with you for this day's business, young lord, you'll see," he muttered.

As Andrew Brown rowed the two boys back to the Sand Haven he spoke straightly to James. "It does not do to be taking much notice of the fightings and bickerings in the pit. It makes for more trouble in the end. Yon lass, Isobel Norrie, is one o' a family of gipsies that have settled in Culross and come to work at the mines. The mother worked in the mines afore, when she was a bairn, and she knows how to work, but the father and some o' the bairns are right work-dodgers. I leave Ann Norrie to keep her family in order, and I don't interfere."

"What about the lad?" James asked, frowning. "He shouldn't be allowed to ill-treat a lass."

"John Horne? Weel, maybe she got in his way. The Hornes have worked in the Moat Pit ever since it was dug. They're a Culross family and good workers, if a bit dour. Isn't there one of the womenfolk serves at the big house, Edward?"

"Yes. John Horne's elder sister, Bessie, helps in the kitchen. She's a sour-faced lass." Edward made a grimace. He spoke shortly and returned all at once to something about which James had spoken earlier. "You know, Andrew, James is right. There would be fewer bickerings and accidents if we could bring the coal out of the mines by machinery instead of by bearers. You've given me an idea, James. Maybe we could work something out together? You are good at mathematics and I know something about machinery. Then some day I'll put *my* machinery in this pit."

The two cousins smiled at each other with friendly understanding.

Andrew pulled alongside the quay and fastened the boat. As the boys climbed out they were hailed by a smaller boy, fair-haired, like all the Bruces of Culross. "Edward! Edward! Where have you been till now?"

"Oh! Plague take it! There's my brother Alexander. What does *he* want?" Edward muttered.

Alexander pointed accusingly at the boat. "You've just come from the Moat Pit, Edward. I saw you on the Moat Pit. You've got coal dust on the sleeve of your doublet. Have you been down the mine?"

"Mind your own business!" Edward said curtly.

"You have! You have! You can't deny it. You know Grandmother does not like us to go down the mine. What will she say when she finds you have disobeyed her?"

"Are you going to be a Tell-Tale again?" Edward said, with a menacing gleam in his eye. Alexander drew back a little. "Isn't it enough that you got Magdalen into trouble on Sunday?" Edward went on. "Why must you always go toadying to my grandmother with tales? Can't you keep your tongue still?" Edward turned to James. "Never trust this one with anything you do not want my grandmother to know," he added with contempt.

Alexander went scurrying away, head held down. The other two followed at a more leisurely pace to the big house at the Sand Haven. "Always there is trouble with my grandmother!" Edward said bitterly.

CHAPTER 4

A WORK OF MERCY

THE Bruce children received lessons from Mr. Robert Colville, the minister at the Abbey Church of Culross, who lived in the minister's house at the top of the Tanhouse Brae, known as the manse. Every morning he came to give the children instruction, including the girls, for Sir George Bruce gave orders that the girls were to be taught to read and write and to cast up figures as well as the boys.

"A waste of time! They'd be better employed learning how to make butter and bake bread, and to spin and use a needle," Lady Bruce declared. "Learning to cast up accounts will never get them husbands!" But her husband insisted on his own way.

"The lasses must be educated as well as the lads. Ignorant women are like a lot of magpies chattering in a house. There will be plenty of time for them to learn spinning in the afternoon," he declared, so each morning the girls who were old enough joined the boys in the schoolroom.

Robert Colville was tall and gaunt, with a hooked nose and a stern expression. In his black woollen doublet and hose and black cape he seemed to James Bruce just like a large raven. He carried an ash plant walking-stick with which he rapped the knuckles of any child whose attention wandered. His glittering eye fixed James with a curious expression.

"So we have a new cousin come to live with us, eh?" It was plainly a question that did not need an answer, so James clicked his heels and made a polite bow in his continental style. Mr. Colville raised his eyebrows. "Ah! I heard we had lived abroad," he commented. Evidently "we" was intended to refer to James in a slightly mocking way. "Well, let us see what we have learned during our residence in Europe. Have you the Latin, boy?" he bellowed suddenly.

"I hope I have, sir. I was instructed in Latin by the good brothers of the Franciscan monastery at Padua."

"Ha!" Colville snorted. "I hope the Romish brothers did not instruct you in their Romish faith too." His voice was full of hatred, and James did not reply. "Whatever you have learned, remember I shall expect you to be in your place at the Abbey Church on the Sabbath."

"Have no fear, sir. I shall be there with my cousins," James assured him pleasantly. "In any case I am of my father's religion, and he loved the Abbey Church of Culross all his days."

Colville gave him a quick questioning look. "And who was your father? If he visited the Abbey often, I should have known him."

Too late James remembered the promise to Sir George Bruce to say nothing of his father and to conceal his identity. He could have bitten his tongue out. Edward pulled a face to caution him.

"He was a Bruce—a distant kinsman to Sir George. He visited Culross when he was a child, and he never forgot the happy days he spent there," James told Colville. "But you were asking about my studies when I made a remark that was out of place and interrupted you."

The conversation about James's father was so quietly and politely closed that Robert Colville had no chance of making more inquiries without seeming inquisitive. "Well, your Latin? What have you read?"

"All Caesar's commentaries, sir, and most of the books of Virgil, Horace's odes and Plutarch's histories."

"Mm!" Colville made a non-committal snort. This lad was further advanced than his own pupils.

"I have some Greek too," James went on, "though I am not very able in that yet. For other languages I speak Italian and French——"

"Spare us the catalogue of your learning till it is asked," Robert Colville spoke with heavy sarcasm. "What of your progress in the sciences? Mathematics, now?"

"He is further advanced in Euclid than I am, sir," Edward spoke up generously.

"Hold your tongue, boy. The lad can speak for himself," Colville said sourly. "What other accomplishments have you, young sir? Astronomy, now? Is the Astronomer Royal likely to give up his place to you?"

James decided to treat this jeer as a joke and laughed heartily. "Oh, no, sir! I have not learned much about the stars yet. No doubt you will be able to teach me much more."

Colville hastily changed the subject. "What else have you studied?"

"A—a little chemistry, sir."

"Chemistry?" Colville barked. "Chemistry? An invention of the Evil One, akin to witchcraft."

"No, I assure you, sir. There are good uses for chemistry."

"Do not contradict me, lad, or you'll taste my stick," Colville thundered. "We'll have no more mention of chemistry, if you please. What other branches of science have you pursued?" There was no mistaking the sneering tone of the question.

James squirmed a little. "One of the brothers at Padua taught me about plants and herbs, sir, and how they can be used as medicine. He—he—was very learned in the matter——" he faltered before Colville's contemptuous eye.

"Plants and herbs? Leave those to the old wives and witches who want to make a poultice or a purging brew. Here you will receive no such frivolous instruction."

James flushed to the roots of his hair and looked about to reply angrily, then snapped his mouth shut.

"Well, well! We must waste no further time. You and Edward can construe a Horace Ode for me. I will give you a few moments to look it over while I hear Magdalen recite her catechism. Alexander, you can go on with your writing copy."

"I have been employed on it, sir, while you were talking to my Cousin James," Alexander said smugly.

"Good boy! At least you have not been like the rest, gaping idly and wasting time," Colville frowned at the other children, but he had a special smile for Alexander.

"Latin! Latin! Latin! I'm fair sick of Latin. I'd rather be at the mathematics," Edward whispered to James under cover of Magdalen's droning of the catechism. Down came Mr. Colville's stick smartly on both their knuckles!

"No chattering! Get on with your work."

"Oh, sir! James never spoke at all." Edward indignantly shouldered the blame.

"Enough, boy! Down to your Latin!"

The boys bent their heads to their task in silence but Robert

Colville threw them an uneasy glance. It was plain they were firm friends, united in a bond against him now. Who was this boy who had come to Culross from Europe? Colville frowned and completely overlooked a mistake that Magdalen made in her sing-song recital. When Lady Bruce had told him he was to have another pupil for a time, she had mentioned that a young kinsman had arrived "with his great-aunt" and the corners of her mouth had been drawn down in disapproval. Who could the great-aunt be? Robert Colville cast his mind back through the generations of Bruces he had known, and he could not identify the 'great-aunt' with any of them. And the lad was not fair like the Bruces, but with the large dark eyes of an Italian. Italy? The boy had been educated in Padua, he said. There was no Bruce whom Robert Colville knew who had been in Padua. Here was a mystery he was determined to solve. A little pressure on the lad, perhaps, might reveal the truth? He was brought back from his musings by Magdalen's droning fading into silence. She was looking at him with a quizzical expression.

"Sharpen your quill and get on with your writing copy," he bellowed.

"If you please, sir"—she dropped him a slightly mocking curtsy—"my grandfather said he would have me learn how to write household accounts."

Robert Colville gave an exclamation of annoyance. "Wenches would be better employed in the household than in casting up figures."

"Then shall I tell my grandfather that, sir?" she asked in a voice of childish innocence, but Colville knew well enough she was baiting him.

"Hold your tongue, you impudent besom!" he said in anger. "Get on with your writing till I bid you to stop." He turned to Alexander and his voice and his expression softened as he passed his hand over the boy's fair curls. "Now, my laddie, we will hear your Latin verbs."

The boy began to repeat the words in a glib sure voice.

"Alexander?" Robert Colville put the question to himself. Alexander would tell him all he wanted to know. He looked up to find Magdalen glancing from him to Alexander as though she read his thoughts.

While their children were at their lessons Barbara Ruthven

helped Mary Preston, the younger George Bruce's wife, at the spinning. This was done in a small back room which looked down across a narrow lane to some cottages built almost in the shadow of Sir George Bruce's house. Below them, too, was a well to which people were constantly coming with buckets and ewers.

"That's Bessie Barr's well. It's got the best and cleanest water in Culross," Mary told Lady Barbara.

"Who is Bessie Barr?" Barbara asked.

"Oh, she *was* the widow of a man who traded in malt, and she lived in that biggish house across the lane. She carried on her husband's trade and she died quite a wealthy woman. The house is called Bessie Barr's Lodging still, and the crag up above the garden is named Bessie Barr's Hagg too."

Barbara leaned out of the window. "Who lives there now?" she asked idly.

"The house belongs to Sir George now. He divided it into two parts, an upper and a lower one. Andrew Brown, his overseer at the mine, lives in the lower half. The upper part is empty just now, but I think Lady Bruce has half promised it to John Kerr, the webster. It would be handy to have someone close by to weave cloth for the household."

The two spinning-wheels whirred for a while, with Mary only pausing now and again to push the cradle with her foot. In it was her youngest child, another Mary.

"In the summer I take the spinning-wheel out to the terraced garden behind the houses. It is peaceful and pleasant and the high crags keep off the cold winds. I long for the warmer days when the pear blossom forms in tight clusters on the stone wall."

"You love this place, then, Mary?"

"I *could* love it very much if—if it were not for my mother-in-law's overbearing ways. Perhaps it seems strange to you that this place should mean so much to me, you who have travelled so far and seen so much, and I have never been farther than Perth and Edinburgh."

"I have a love for Scotland, too, Mary, or I should not have come back. I still think there is no lovelier sight than the blue waters of the Firth of Forth dancing in the sun, and the smoky mist across the Firth over the red roofs of Edinburgh, with the green hills of the Pentlands rising behind them and the shadows of the clouds chasing across the hills."

"Why, then, did you stay away so long?"

The humming of the spinning-wheels drowned all other sounds, and neither of them noticed Alexander quietly open the door and come into the room. He heard his mother's question and stood still in the shadow, watching the play of the firelight upon their faces.

"Because I was an exile, Mary. I dared not come back."

Mary started. "But *why*, Barbara? What wrong could you have done anyone, who are so gentle and kind?"

"I have had to learn gentleness in a hard school, Mary. Even now the fiery temper of the Ruthvens rises in black anger in me when my pride is hurt."

"Were you kin to—to——?" Mary hardly liked to speak the name.

"To the Earl of Ruthven whom King James accused of an attempt on his life? Yes. He was my brother. But while I am in this house I am to go under the name of Mistress Barbara Bruce, lest my real name should bring discredit on the family." Barbara spoke with bitterness.

"My husband told me you had come back for the sake of James."

"Yes. But I fear there is small hope of getting his claim recognized to the Kinloss lands." Barbara shook her head sadly. "The present Lord Kinloss stands too high in the King's favour for right to be done, and we have no money to pay lawyers."

"Lord Kinloss is in England now, at the court," Mary told her. "The great house up the Tanhouse Brae is empty."

"Then we cannot even go and appeal to Lord Kinloss himself. But he is hardly likely to give up his estates to James without a fight, and I fear the law courts might not take my word for it that James is the lawful son of the Lord Edward Kinloss who was killed in a duel nigh on thirteen years ago."

"Perhaps God will show you what to do," Mary said in her simple faith.

"I pray so, for I hardly know where to turn." Barbara bent over her spinning-wheel and its hum rose higher. Quietly Alexander let himself out of the room again, closing the door gently behind him. Barbara felt a draught of cold air and looked up quickly, but the door had already closed.

"It should be time for the children to finish their lessons. They generally seek me out here. I—I keep a few sweetmeats for them in this sewing box," Mary confessed with a laugh. Almost as if they had heard her, Edward, Magdalen and James came in.

"Well, how did the lessons go?" Mary Bruce asked.

"Oh, much as usual. We got a very skimpy lesson in mathematics, and endless Latin," Edward complained. "I begin to think that Mr. Colville knows little but Latin."

"And James confounded him with a question in mathematics," Magdalen giggled.

"Ssh! Don't let Alexander carry that tale back to Mr. Colville," Edward warned her.

"Safe enough! Alexander isn't here," Magdalen snorted.

"Where is he then? I thought he'd have been here long before, eating up all the sweetmeats. Mr. Colville let him go before the rest of us, for good conduct, he said," Edward told them.

"No. He hasn't been here. I'd better lay some comfits aside for him." His mother was just doing this when Alexander sidled into the room.

"Hullo! Where have you been?" Edward demanded.

"Taking a message to the kitchen for my grandmother," Alexander said smoothly, "and while I was there Bessie Horne gave me an oatcake and some milk."

"Ah! That's why he's so pleased to take messages to the kitchen," Magdalen snorted. "Bessie Horne's little pet lamb."

Alexander scowled at her.

The name Horne reminded James of the quarrel he had seen at the Moat Pit and the invitation he had given to Isobel Norrie to come to his aunt to have her arm dressed. He poured out the story in Barbara Ruthven's ear. "So I told her you would look to her arm if she asked for you by name. Was that all right, Aunt Barbara?"

She looked a little troubled. "What name did you give her?"

"I told her Mistress Barbara Bruce."

"I will do what I can for the child if she comes here," she promised.

Alexander looked from one to the other inquisitively. He did not understand all that had passed between his mother and Mistress Barbara, but he could remember their words. James's story was quite plain to him, though. James had asked a dirty gipsy girl out of the mine to come to the house. She had been fighting John Horne. That news would not please his grandmother, nor Bessie Horne either.

It was not till the dusk was falling that Isobel Norrie came timidly gliding along by the shadows to the first of the great houses. She hesitated by the gate into the forecourt, afraid to enter, and waited for a time beneath the elm tree. Then, summoning up courage, she advanced to the flight of steps. From the porter's lodge at the foot, under the shadow of the stone balcony, old Henry hailed her. "Wha's that? What's wanted?"

"I—I was told to come to see Mistress Barbara Bruce," Isobel stammered.

Henry held his lantern higher and peered at her. He saw the coal grime streaking her face, though she had made an attempt to wash herself with the sea-water, and her hair was matted and her clothes tattered.

"Awa' wi' you, you dirty wean! What do you mean by sneaking round the doors of noblemen's houses? I ken who you are. One o' they thievin' gipsies from the shore," he shouted at her. "Be off!" He raised his stick.

Isobel shrank back afraid. "But the laddie who was with Master Edward told me to come," she protested.

"You lying young scamp! You're just after what you can lay your hands on." Henry caught her by the shoulder and would have run her out at the gate, but suddenly his arm was held from behind. He faced about quickly, fearing an attack, but it was only Magdalen who held him by the sleeve.

"Let go of her, Henry! Let go of the girl at once, I say!" Magdalen ordered him furiously.

"Why? What ails you, Mistress Magdalen? Would you have me let a rascally wench from the mine inside the house?"

"Did you not hear what she said to you? That my Cousin James had bidden her to come to see Mistress Barbara Bruce?"

"A likely story! What would Mistress Barbara or anyone else be wanting wi' a dirty-faced lass like yon?"

"It's *true*, I tell you! I heard James tell Mistress Barbara about her. *Now* will you let her pass?"

"No, no, little mistress! I'll go away quietly. I do not want to get into trouble," Isobel Norrie told her in a trembling voice.

"You'll do no such thing! You'll come with me as I bid you. Stand aside, Henry!" Magdalen commanded.

"I don't know who gives me orders these days," Henry grumbled to a woman who appeared from the kitchen. "Yon Mistress Magdalen is a right vixen."

Bessie Horne curled her lip vindictively as the two girls sped across the forecourt to the larger house where Barbara Ruthven had her room.

"Up the stairs with you quickly, before anyone else sees us!" Magdalen ordered. She paused only to rap on the door of Lady Barbara's apartment.

"Come in!" Barbara's voice invited them. Magdalen drew Isobel in with her and closed the door.

"This is the collier lass James told you about," she said.

"Oh, yes. My nephew said you had hurt your arm." Lady Barbara spoke gently to the girl who shrank back and pulled her tattered shawl closer about her.

"I shouldna be here! I shouldna be here!" she whispered in a frightened voice. "Let me go, mistress, afore I get a thrashing for daring to come to this place."

"Let me see your arm first. Come now, there is nothing to fear. No one will hurt you."

Isobel Norrie crept a step or two nearer to her, then threw back her shawl and rolled up her tattered sleeve. The wound was thick with coal dust and grime and dried blood, and an angry inflamed line was plain to be seen. Though Barbara Ruthven handled it gently, the girl cringed when her arm was touched.

"This arm must have some care at once. Already it is swollen and badly inflamed," Barbara declared. "I shall need some hot water, Magdalen. Do you think you could get me a ewer from the kitchen?"

"No, no, mistress! Pray let my arm be. It will heal of itself in no time. I have had other wounds before that have healed," Isobel begged her.

"Not this one! There is poison from dirt in the wound already. Do you want to lose your arm, silly lass?"

"Oh, no, no!" Isobel sounded terrified.

Henry held his lantern higher and peered at her

"Then you must let me tend it."

"I'll go to the kitchen for the hot water, Aunt Barbara. There is bound to be some in the big iron cauldron," Magdalen said.

While Magdalen was away Barbara Ruthven opened the lid of the wooden chest containing her belongings and brought out a pair of scissors, some strips of clean linen and a small box which contained some salve.

Magdalen rushed across the forecourt to the kitchen. There, above the smouldering embers of the great fire hung a great cauldron in which water simmered.

"A pitcher of that hot water, please, Bessie Horne," she demanded.

"And what for should I be giving you water from the cauldron?" Bessie Horne asked impertinently.

Magdalen looked her straight in the eye. "Because Mistress Barbara Bruce requires it."

"What does she want it for?"

"That is *her* business. I'll thank you to fill a pitcher for me, Bessie Horne, or I will go to my mother and tell her of your impudence."

"Oh, hoity-toity!" Bessie Horne tossed her head, but nevertheless she reached a pitcher from a hook on a shelf and dipped it into the cauldron. "Don't think I didn't see you hobnobbing wi' yon dirty gipsy lass Norrie out o' the mines. Your grandmother would not be o'er pleased at that."

"Mind your own business! It will become you better, Bessie Horne." Magdalen rebuked her with the dignity of one far beyond her age. She took the pitcher from the woman's reluctant hands and carried it carefully across the forecourt and up the steps of the second house. In another minute she was safe inside Lady Barbara's room with the door closed. She found James had joined his aunt too.

Lady Barbara wasted no time. She dipped a piece of white linen in the steaming hot water and dabbed gently at the wound. Though Isobel winced, she uttered no cry but set her teeth and stood her ground. In a few moments the angry cut across the pink flesh was revealed. Lady Barbara continued to wash it till every particle of dirt had disappeared. Then she spread salve gently over the edges of the wound and wrapped a clean linen bandage several times round it.

"I ought to tell you not to use it for a few days, but I suppose that is no use?" Lady Barbara asked.

The girl shook her head. "I must take my place down the mine tomorrow, mistress."

"Poor child!" Barbara's voice was full of pity. "Then you must try to keep the wound as clean as you can. If I could find some wild thyme, a brew from that might help to cleanse it." She spoke half to herself.

The girl's eyes brightened. She asked, "Do you know about herbs, mistress?" It was as though she had found something in common between this fine lady and herself.

"Yes, I have some knowledge of them, Isobel."

"My grandmother had that knowledge too, but that was when we lived in the woodlands and moors and were free people. Now we are in bondage, and my family have lost their learning about herbs."

"What do you mean by saying that your people are in bondage?" James asked.

"Now we have taken work in the mines we must always work in the mines."

"But why is that?"

Isobel looked surprised at the question. "Do you not know that once a man and his family take work down a mine, they are tied to the same master as long as they live?"

"But that is a kind of slavery!" James exclaimed indignantly.

"What she says is true. No miner can leave my grandfather's service unless my grandfather gives him permission," Magdalen supported Isobel's statement.

"Yes, I have heard that is the law," Lady Barbara nodded. "Miners' families must always work in the mine where their fathers take service."

"If we run away, we can be thrashed and brought back again. It is true that since we worked in the mine we have a roof over our heads and we can now buy meal for porridge and barley bread, but I liked it better when we were free and slept under the stars. Then we did not have to toil, day in, day out, up and down the ladders in the mine," the girl suddenly put her hand to her mouth as if she had said too much. "I—I am sorry, mistress. I could be punished for what I have said——"

"Have no fear! No one here will repeat what you have

said," Lady Barbara assured her. "Tomorrow you must come to me again and have that arm dressed. Perhaps, in the meantime, I might find some violet leaves or the roots of the red docken——" Again it seemed as if she were thinking aloud.

"I can take you to the places where they might be found if my mother will spare me from the spinning tomorrow afternoon," Magdalen told her confidently.

"That is kind of you, Magdalen. Tomorrow evening, after your work in the mine is done, come and ask for me again, Isobel."

"Yes, my lady." Isobel Norrie made a little bobbing curtsy and turned to go, then staggered with a sudden faintness and would have fallen but for James who caught her by the arm and assisted her to a chair.

"Do you feel ill, child?" Lady Barbara asked anxiously.

Isobel shook her head. "No, no! I just turned queer and dizzy——"

It was Magdalen who knew what was wrong. "Have you had anything to eat since you left the mine?"

Isobel shook her head.

"Sit there, then. I'll bring you something," Magdalen said. She rushed off to the kitchen again. A large cauldron of broth was simmering on the fire for Sir George's supper, and quickly Magdalen ladled some into a bowl and snatched some oatcake from a cupboard.

"What are you doing, Mistress Magdalen?" Bessie Horne demanded, as she came into the kitchen in time to see Magdalen whisking out by another door.

"Feeding the hungry as it tells us in the Scriptures," she retorted, and before Bessie could think of a reply, she had disappeared across the courtyard again.

Warmed by the good beef broth and the oatcake, Isobel soon recovered and the colour came back into her cheeks. "Thank you, Mistress Barbara Bruce, and you too, Mistress Magdalen. I have not eaten so well for many a long day." A friendly glance of understanding passed between the two girls. "If ever I can be of service to you, I will," Isobel promised them quietly. "I shall not forget your kindness."

She slipped away down the stairs and across the forecourt, still keeping to the shadows, and down the sandy lane to the damp stone hut on the shore that was her home. Unknown to her, from the shelter of old Henry's watch-post Bessie Horne saw her and shook her fist.

"There she goes! A right besom, that one! She tried to get my brother into trouble at the mine with yon Master James, whoever he might be!" she sniffed.

"Who is this Mistress Barbara? I heard someone call her Lady Barbara, too," old Henry said curiously.

"More than you would like to know that! I wonder where they came from."

"Off a Dutch ship. *I* can tell you that," old Henry replied.

"Then I wish they'd go back. Extra work they make, and Mistress Magdalen is getting right impudent, coming to the kitchen and demanding this and that for their gipsy friend. Hot water, forsooth! And *I've* got to pump the water and fill the cauldron! Well, we'll see what Lady Bruce has to say to such on-goings." Bessie Horne stamped furiously back to her kitchen.

The next afternoon, with Magdalen to guide her, Barbara Ruthven set off with a basket over her arm and collected wild herbs from the hedgerows and marshy fields by the foreshore. From some plants she took the shoots and leaves, but she dug up the roots of others with a sharp knife.

"What do you do with the herbs?" Magdalen asked, as she helped her.

"Some of the leaves I dry slowly, then rub them to powder; the roots I dry, too, and scrape them finely. Some powders I dissolve in water for medicine; others I mix with lard to make ointments. Every herb has its use. With some I can cure fevers; with others I can heal wounds, and others still are good for coughs, and some herbs can give sleep to those whose minds are sick."

Magdalen looked at Barbara with a great respect. "But how did you learn what herbs to give for different sicknesses?"

"My brother taught me when I was young. We have always had a skill with herbs in our family. Even James knows the different uses almost as well as I do."

"James?" Magdalen sounded surprised. "Why, yes, he did tell Mr. Colville that one of the monks at Padua had taught him about plants and herbs. Mr. Colville told him to leave that knowledge to the old wives and witches."

Barbara Ruthven flushed with annoyance. "Mr. Colville was wrong to speak like that to James. James might become a great doctor. He has the gift of healing like many of the Ruthvens had."

"The Ruthvens? But I thought James was a Bruce?" Magdalen looked puzzled.

"Yes, he is a Bruce on his father's side. Forget what I said about the Ruthvens, Magdalen, and mention that name to no one, I beg you." Barbara looked troubled.

"I will keep my tongue still," Magdalen promised. "Bessie Horne's mother, old Elspeth, pretends to heal people and sometimes uses herbs, but she has no knowledge as you have. She uses charms and spells and some folk say she is a witch. The farmers sometimes ask her for a charm to cure their sick cows, and sometimes the sailors pay her a penny to raise a wind for them." Magdalen looked anxiously at Barbara Ruthven. "You are not a witch, are you, Aunt Barbara?"

Barbara smiled at her. "No, Magdalen, I am not a witch, though it is sometimes given to me to know things that other people do not." Magdalen looked puzzled and Barbara took her by the shoulders and faced her round. "Listen to me, child. A herb that God made can be used for healing or for witchcraft. There are always two ways of using God's gifts, for good or for evil. To heal the sick by God's gift of herbs is good; to make spells and enchantments is stupid and wicked. Remember that always."

The child looked at her inspired, her face glowing. "Will you teach me your skill with herbs too, Aunt Barbara, as you taught James?"

"Yes, if your mother is willing, and if—if we are long enough here," Barbara agreed. Misgiving suddenly filled her heart with strange premonitions. "We have gathered enough herbs now. Let us go back. I want to make a fomentation of these comfrey leaves to lay on Isobel's arm and draw any poison from the wound. Do you think you could ask for hot water from the kitchen for me again?"

"Oh, yes, I will do that, though Bessie Horne is right dour," Magdalen laughed. "I am not her pet like Alexander is."

CHAPTER 5

BESSIE BARR'S LODGING

THAT night when Isobel Norrie came again, Magdalen was watching for her through the window. As soon as she saw Isobel slip through the gate, she ran down the short flight of stone steps and intercepted her before old Henry could turn her away. As the two girls crossed the forecourt, Henry scowled after them.

"Am I the watchman or am I no'?" he asked himself. "Yon chit of a lass, Mistress Magdalen, seems to have taken my duties on herself. Weel, perhaps Lady Bruce will have something to say about that."

A few minutes later Magdalen sped down the stairs to the kitchen for hot water. As she dipped the pitcher in the cauldron, Bessie Horne came out of the bakehouse.

"What are you doing, Mistress Magdalen?" she asked sharply.

"Just taking hot water for Mistress Barbara, Bessie."

"I canna spare it," Bessie told her. "I'll need the water to boil the fish for supper and the rest of it for washing the dishes afterwards."

"Och, you'll never miss a pitcher full! There'll be plenty of time to draw more at the well and fill up the cauldron and get it boiling again before supper."

"I'm not spending my time drawing water up the well just to waste it on yon gipsy wench." Bessie's temper was getting the better of her, but Magdalen seized the pitcher and said haughtily, "Remember your place, Bessie Horne. Please to open the door for me."

"We'll see what your grandmother has to say to these cantrips," Bessie threatened as Magdalen passed her.

Lady Barbara fomented Isobel's arm with water, as hot as Isobel could bear, in which the comfrey leaves had been steeped. As she did it, she chatted to Isobel to take her mind off the pain. "Are there many children in the mine who suffer from cuts and bruises like yours, Isobel?"

"Oh, aye, mistress, we all do."

"And does no one doctor them?"

Isobel shook her head. "No one bothers about them. If they heal up, they do it of themselves. If they do not——" she shook her head.

"But with all the dirt of the mine many cuts must get poisoned as this one did?"

"Aye, sometimes bairns swell up and die when they've had an injury. Many of them have running sores that will not heal. But what's to be done, mistress?"

"The wounds could at least be washed and kept clean. Is there nobody to care for you bairns?"

"Nobody except those in our homes. When my mother's been down the mine all day, her legs swell too, and she canna be bothered wi' us bairns." Isobel accepted this conduct as a matter of course.

"Something ought to be done for the children of the mine when they're hurt, Aunt Barbara." James leaned forward urgently from the corner where he had been sitting watching his aunt's skilful fingers. "Couldn't we do something?"

Barbara Ruthven turned to him. "What could we do, James?"

"What you are doing now for Isobel—washing and binding up their wounds and healing them with salves and herbs. I would help you."

Barbara gave a beautiful smile at his eagerness.

"Listen, Aunt Barbara, please," he went on. "If Isobel could bring the little ones here—those who can do little for themselves—we could try to heal them. There are others, too, perhaps, who are ill . . ."

"There are many of us who are sick—some of us cough day and night from the coal dust—some children have pains in their legs and swollen feet from standing all day in the mud and water of the mine. There are some nigh blinded, too, with sore eyes," Isobel told them.

"Perhaps we might do something to help them, if Isobel would bring them here one or two at a time," Barbara Ruthven began.

"I would like to help too. Many of the children know me,"
Magdalen began.

Just then there was a sharp rap at the door and Lady Bruce
walked in. Quickly the children sprang to their feet and Magdalen made her curtsy. Barbara Ruthven followed suit with
dignity. Lady Bruce looked them all up and down with a cool
disapproving stare without speaking at first. Then she pointed
to Isobel, her nostrils lifting with disdain.

"What is that dirty gipsy brat doing in my house?"

Barbara Ruthven flushed. "Your pardon, my lady. She is a
poor child from the mine. Her arm has been badly cut and I was
fomenting it with herbs."

"Herbs?" Lady Bruce sniffed contemptuously. "We leave
those to the old wives and the apothecaries at the fair." She
turned with annoyance to Magdalen. "What is this I hear from
Bessie Horne that you take water from her kitchen so that she
cannot get on with preparing the supper? Nay, now, no impertinent answer! And Henry the watchman complains that
you give him orders, and tell him whom he is to admit to the
house."

"It was only this poor girl, Grandmother," Magdalen began
to protest.

"Understand, Magdalen, that I will not have filthy, evil-
smelling children from the mines brought into my house."

"It was my fault, Lady Bruce. I asked Isobel Norrie to come
here to let my aunt tend her arm."

"*You* asked her to come? By what right? You make free with
my house, young sir!" Lady Bruce spoke indignantly.

"I am sorry—I did not think——" James began to stutter in
dismay, when Barbara Ruthven intervened.

"We should have asked your permission first, my lady. I
realize that now and I ask your pardon. We did not mean to
be discourteous. It was just that a work of mercy was required
of us."

"*I* am the best judge of what works of mercy are required in
Culross," Lady Bruce told her in icy tones. "Have I not lived
here all my life and know the people better than any new in-
comer?"

Barbara Ruthven's eyes blazed with anger, but she pressed
her lips together.

"I know the Norrie family for the idle thieving gipsies they are." Lady Bruce turned to the girl. "Be gone with you, wench, and don't dare to show your dirty face here again, or I'll have you whipped."

Isobel Norrie turned and fled down the stairs like a hunted animal.

"It would be better, James, if you did not interfere in the quarrels between the children in the mines in future. Remember you are a visitor here." Her glance took in Lady Barbara, as if she would include her in the reminder. James made her a courteous bow but did not speak. Lady Barbara's eyes met those of Lady Bruce and held them. It was Lady Bruce, who, disconcerted, dropped her gaze first. Proudly she swept from the room.

When she was out of earshot Magdalen said furiously, "I wonder who told my grandmother of the quarrel between Isobel Norrie and John Horne? I *hate* Bessie Horne."

James looked very troubled. "Does that mean you will not be able to look after Isobel Norrie's arm again, Aunt Barbara?"

"I fear it does, James."

"And that other children from the mines will not be able to come here?"

"We have no right to ask them. We are but guests here ourselves, and not very welcome guests at that, I fear."

"Then we must give up our plan to doctor the children from the mine?" James asked.

"So long as we stay in this house, yes."

"How long shall we be staying here?" James asked unhappily. He did not want to leave his new-found cousins, but he knew it would no longer be comfortable for either of them to stay long in the house with Lady Bruce.

"We must stay at Culross till we have accomplished the purpose for which we came." Barbara Ruthven looked determined. "We are not going to be frightened away by cold looks when we have been here less than a week. We shall see what happens next."

When Lady Bruce left the crestfallen little group behind her, she went straight to her husband in his business room in the old house. It was a specially strong room with double doors and thicker walls, built off the bedroom, where Sir George could keep his gold protected. Before the days of banks in Scotland, men of wealth had to devise means of safeguarding their valuables. Lady Bruce knew they were unlikely to be overheard here. She closed both doors behind her.

"Something must be done about that woman. I will have her no longer in my house," she declared, heated with temper.

"What woman?" Sir George asked a little wearily, lifting his head from the papers and account books spread out on the table before him.

"Why, Barbara Ruthven, of course! She has been in this place less than a week and already she has upset the servants and encouraged Magdalen in frowardness and impertinence. Now the latest thing is that she is inviting dirty children from the mine to her room. *That* I will not endure!"

"Children from the mine? How many children?" he rapped out.

"Well, one of them," she had to admit. "Isobel Norrie, one of a dirty thieving family of tinkers who have come to work in the mine. Bessie Horne knows of her."

"But why should she bring a child from the mine into the house?" Sir George was plainly puzzled.

"Under the guise of charity, to bind up a cut arm, but you never know what plots a Ruthven might be hatching."

"Surely not with a little gipsy wench?" Sir George reasoned temperately.

"Laugh at me if you like, but you know well enough that King James would not be over-pleased that you should harbour the sister of his bitterest enemy in your house."

Sir George was silent. There was something in what his wife said. James VI had a long memory for his enemies.

"You have risen high in the King's esteem already, George. He has knighted you. He has even honoured this house with his presence, and might do so again when he comes to Scotland. Who knows what honour he might bestow next time? But not if it is whispered in his ear that you have given house-room to a Ruthven. Would you throw away what you have gained for that?"

Sir George Bruce was an ambitious man. He knew his wife might be right. "What's to be done, then?"

"Turn her out," Lady Bruce said promptly.

"I cannot do that. I promised her shelter, and I will not

go back on my word, for she and the boy are penniless."

Lady Bruce snorted in contempt and anger.

"Besides, the boy is a kinsman and has claims on me," he went on. "I like the lad too."

"I will not endure her any longer——" Lady Bruce was beginning when Sir George held up his hand.

"Wait! I think I can see a way round the difficulty that will satisfy my honour and your anger. She shall not reside any longer under this roof."

Lady Bruce had begun to preen herself in triumph when Sir George went on, "But I must give her shelter and hospitality as I promised. There is room in the house that once belonged to Bessie Barr. She can go there with the boy."

Lady Bruce's face fell with dismay. "Bessie Barr's Lodging? But that is next to us!"

"All the better to keep an eye on her."

"But—but I promised the rooms to John Kerr, the weaver. I cannot go back on my word now," she exclaimed.

"Neither can I go back on my word to Barbara Ruthven. It must be either Bessie Barr's old house, or this. You must choose which way you will have it, wife."

Lady Bruce knew well when she had reached the end of her husband's patience. "All right, then. It will have to be Bessie Barr's Lodging," she gave in sulkily. "It is not likely to be for long, anyway," she added darkly.

"I will speak to Barbara Ruthven in the parlour after supper," Sir George decided.

Supper was a quiet meal that night, with little talk among the company. Sir George seemed ill at ease and from time to time passed his hand across his brow with a weary gesture. Lady Bruce wore an aloof air. The children were quiet and subdued.

A manservant spoke in Lady Barbara's ear. "Sir George says he would like a word with you in the parlour after supper, if you please, mistress."

Sir George rose and placed a seat for Lady Barbara when she entered the parlour. Lady Bruce inclined her head but did not speak. A little sheepishly he told Lady Barbara of his plan to give her the rooms in Betty Barr's Lodging. Rather to his surprise she did not become angry or indignant at this slight, but looked relieved.

"I could look on that lodging as my own home, to do in as I pleased?"

"Yes. You could do that."

"And James could continue to have his lessons with your grandchildren?"

"There would be no objection to that," Sir George agreed.

Lady Bruce added, "Provided he minds his manners and is not impertinent to Mr. Colville."

Barbara threw her an indignant look, but made no retort. Instead she spoke to Sir George. "Then I thank you for your kind offer. I shall be pleased to occupy the house you suggest."

"We will see that the place is furnished suitably, and your belongings shall be moved across to the house tomorrow," Lady Bruce said with some relief.

"Thank you, Lady Bruce. If you will pardon me, I think I shall like this arrangement better than having an apartment in your big house, where perhaps my presence is an embarrassment to you," Barbara Ruthven said frankly. Both Sir George and Lady Bruce looked uncomfortable, but Barbara went on, "Besides, I too have always liked my freedom. Thank you, Sir George. Thank you, my lady." Lady Barbara made them a sweeping curtsy and passed out of the room.

"That's over, thank goodness," Sir George said with relief. "She took it pretty well."

"She had no choice. But I wish she was out of Culross altogether. Never trust a Ruthven!" Lady Bruce declared.

The next day old Henry carried across Lady Barbara's boxes to the two rooms in the upper storey of Bessie Barr's old house. They were approached by a flight of stone steps from a narrow street. The windows looked towards the Firth. James looked out of the windows with pleasure.

"We can still watch the Firth and all the ships, as we could in Sir George's house," he said.

Barbara stood looking, with her hand on his shoulder. "Yes, James, let us be thankful we have a home of our own. It is next to the well, so we can easily draw our water, and we have a hearth and a fire-basket, aye, and a cauldron too, to heat the water." There was a wealth of meaning in Lady Barbara's voice.

James opened his eyes wide. "You mean we could still go on tending the hurt children?"

"Perhaps, yes, if we go quietly about it, but you must get into no more disputes with lads like John Horne."

James looked unhappy. "It was because of that we got into trouble with Lady Bruce. John Horne is brother to Bessie Horne in the kitchen, so Magdalen told me, and she took a tale to Lady Bruce. It was my fault, Aunt Barbara, that we had to come here and this insult was shown you."

"Don't be troubled about that, James. It merely served Lady Bruce as an excuse for the thing she has been wanting to do ever since I showed my face here. We owe this house to the kindness of Sir George Bruce. Let us make the best of it. We can start by cleaning it thoroughly." She looked about her in some disgust. "It looks as if the floors have never been scrubbed since Bessie Barr died years ago. Can you see a pail anywhere?"

James found a pail upturned in a corner of the next room and went to fetch water from the well. Barbara Ruthven stared about her. The furniture was of the poorest; a deal table on trestles; two stools; some chipped and cracked earthenware, and a low pallet bed in the corner with a pillow and two grey blankets. Barbara crossed the passage to the other smaller room. It held only one stool and another pallet bed. She gave a bitter laugh. "Lady Bruce said the house would be *suitably* furnished. At least we must be thankful for a roof over our heads."

While James was at the well with the bucket, she built a fire with logs and kindling on the hearth and lighted it with the flint and tinder she found on the table. Other footsteps than James's sounded on the stone steps outside.

"We have visitors, Aunt Barbara," James said cheerfully as he came in with the bucket. Behind him on the threshold were Edward and Magdalen and with them a tall well-built man.

"This is Andrew Brown who is overseer to my grandfather's mines. He lives in the house below yours," Edward explained.

"Your pardon, madam. I do not want to intrude on you, but Sir George asked me to tell you that I will see to it that baskets of coal are sent to you each day from the mine."

"Thank you. I shall be glad of the coal," Barbara said gratefully. "And I am grateful to you, too, Andrew Brown, for your visit, seeing we are to be neighbours." She put out her hand and he bowed over it awkwardly, bewitched by all the charm that belonged to the Ruthvens, then he returned down the steps to his own house.

When he was gone Lady Ruthven briskly set about filling the cauldron with water and setting it on the fire. "And now to clean this place," she said.

"Aunt Barbara, please may I stay and help?" Magdalen asked.

"What if you get your clothes dirty?"

"I'll not! I can kilt up my petticoats, and see! I have brought an apron with me."

Barbara laughed at her foresight. "Well, then, shall we begin by scrubbing the furniture?"

"The walls are right dirty too," Magdalen said with distaste. "Listen, Edward, go you with James and beg a pail of limewash from one of the ships' captains, such as the sailors use in the holds of the ships. Don't forget to borrow brushes too. We can find work for you boys as well," she laughed.

The afternoon passed quickly with the slap of whitewash brushes and the sounds of floor washing. At last it was all finished and with the falling of the twilight they looked round with satisfaction at the clean shining rooms.

"My grandmother might at least have sent you some hangings and coverlets for your beds," Magdalen remarked, with a curl of her lip.

"I am content without them," Barbara told her. "Today James and I are starting afresh in our new home."

There was a knock at the door, and when James opened it there stood Isobel Norrie at the top cf the steps with a creel of coal on her back.

"Andrew Brown sent me with this basket of coal to you. He says I am to bring you one every day on my way home from the mines."

"That is very well done by Andrew," James laughed. "Now my aunt will be able to watch the healing of your arm."

"And tomorrow you could bring another child with you to —to help with the coal," Magdalen said with meaning. "And if he or she needs doctoring for a wound or sickness, why, nothing could be simpler."

"Oh, children, children!" Barbara laughed. "Before we know

where we are, you will have turned the place into a hospital. Well, let us begin with Isobel. How is the arm now?"

"Healing well, mistress." She turned up the sleeve and Lady Barbara began to strip off the bandages.

"At least, here we have made a good beginning," she said.

As the days sped by, the upper room in Bessie Barr's Lodging began to look more home-like. Magdalen and her mother, Mary Preston, helped Barbara to weave rush mats for the floors, and Mary brought quilts for the beds and even a tapestry hanging for the blank wall behind the bed. Magdalen brought them candlesticks too, and a supply of candles and wax tapers. These were specially welcome to Barbara Ruthven, for most of the mine-children's timid knocks came to her door after dark.

When the cold winter nights closed in, James fastened the shutters, put coal on the red embers of the fire and lit the candles in their sconces, and, of a sudden, the room looked warm and welcoming. Outside, the tearing gales whipped the black waters of the Forth into fury, but within the little room was comfort and healing for the wretched children who crept there to have their sores tended. Isobel Norrie was their go-between and brought many a child who would not have dared to come alone. Andrew Brown, the overseer, knew of this, living as he did in the ground-floor house below Lady Barbara's, but he said nothing of it to Sir George Bruce. If the children in the mine were better for Mistress Barbara's care of them and could work harder in consequence, then that was all to the good of his master's business. In that stern man there grew a respect for the strange lady who had come to live among them in Culross. Then, one Sabbath day, Andrew's own child, Charles, lay tossing in fever and pain.

"Shall we get old Elspeth Horne to come and cast a charm over the wean?" his wife asked anxiously. Elspeth Horne had a name in Culross for the making of potions and charms.

Andrew looked grim. "Much good that old witch did our William when he lay sick, for all the silver sixpence you gave her! The laddie died just the same."

"What will you do then?" Janet Brown besought him.

"There's Mistress Barbara in the house above. She knows about medicines."

"But she's a grand lady. Would she look at the boy, think you?"

"Wait! I'll see."

Suddenly making up his mind, Andrew strode outside and up the stone stair and rapped at the door above. It was James Bruce who answered it. Andrew's face cleared a little when he saw the lad. "James, you know our laddie, Charles, has been ailing?"

"Yes. Is he any better?"

Andrew shook his head dolefully. "He's far worse, just lying there tossing and whimpering, and we can do nothing for him. The wife's feared we'll lose him as we lost our other son. Do you think Mistress Barbara would——"

Barbara Ruthven heard the conversation and came to the door.

"I am no doctor, you know, Andrew Brown. I cannot let blood, nor do things a doctor might do. I have only a knowledge of herbs and medicines."

"If you'd just come and take a look at him, mistress? You could do more for Charles than the old wife Elspeth Horne did for William when he lay dying," Andrew said bluntly.

"What did she do?" Barbara asked.

"Nothing until the wife first gave her a silver piece of money," Andrew spoke with contempt. "Then she made a wax image of the devil she said had bewitched the laddie, and melted it afore the fire. Much good it did him! When night came, William died, babbling words that no one could tell."

"I shall want no silver piece and I do not make wax images," Barbara Ruthven told him. "But I cannot promise to cure your son, Andrew. That lies only in the hands of God, though I will use what skill I have with medicines. But first I will look at the child."

She and James Bruce followed Andrew down the outer stair to his house.

While Andrew Brown had been talking to Mistress Barbara, Bessie Horne had been clearing away plates in the dining-hall, and she saw him through the window.

"What are you doing at Mistress Barbara Bruce's house, Andrew Brown?" she asked herself curiously. "Someone told me you had a bairn who was sick." When she saw Barbara go down the steps to Andrew's house, her eyes grew narrow. Still she kept her watch by the side of the window. In a few minutes

James Bruce returned alone up the stair, then very shortly re-appeared with Magdalen. Both children were carrying baskets.

"So that is what you are doing, my lady?" Bessie muttered to herself. "Others should know of this." She beckoned a young serving lad aside. "Listen, lad! Go you to my mother at her cottage on the shore and whisper in her ear that there is one at Andrew Brown's house who is taking her place. Tell her to go there to see for herself."

The boy looked puzzled. "Hurry, lad!" she urged him. "When you come back again I'll have oatcake and cheese and ale for you in the kitchen." The boy needed no further prompting, but sped away.

At Andrew Brown's house Barbara Ruthven had found a very sick child indeed. It was plain that he was in a high fever and his breath came in hoarse gasps. Now and again he moaned with pain.

"How long has he been like this?" Lady Barbara asked the boy's mother.

"It was five days ago that he first had fits of shivering and a pain in his chest. Oh, mistress, can you cure him?" Janet Brown begged.

"That, I cannot promise, but I will do what I can. But you must obey exactly every instruction I give you, without question."

"I will do that," the woman promised.

It was then Barbara turned to James, who was looking at the child with great compassion and a curious interest.

"Is it a fever of the lungs, Aunt Barbara?" he asked.

"I think so, James. It has that appearance. Will you go back to our house and bring down all materials to make a poultice?"

"You will want linseed and oil?"

"Yes, and my basket with the phials containing the medicines I have made from herbs. Make sure the one from box leaves is among them."

"You want to make the boy sweat, Aunt Barbara?"

"Yes."

"He is very fevered. Will you not use the medicine made from the leaves of the chestnut too?"

"Yes, bring that phial too, and the one of coltsfoot. That is to soothe the inflammation in the lungs."

James hurried away while his aunt saw to the heating of the water in the cauldron. When he returned, Magdalen was with him.

"I have brought pieces of linen too. James said you wanted to make a poultice," Magdalen said.

"Good girl! First I'll give the distillation from the box leaves. That will soothe him, besides sweating out the fever," Barbara decided. "Have you a cup, please?" she asked Janet Brown.

Into the cup she poured warm water, then dropped several dark drops from the phial. She held it to the boy's lips, supporting him with her arm, and he drank thirstily.

"That will make him sweat," she told his mother, "Do not fear if his skin runs with water. The greater the sweating, the sooner the fever will lessen. Keep giving him sips of warm water. Wrap the blankets well about him, that is all. Then open the window to let fresh air into the room."

"Open the window?" The woman was astonished. "But it's freezing outside!"

"Nevertheless, open the window. The fire has blown smoke into the room and that is bad for his lungs. For this kind of sickness there is nothing better than God's pure air. Now I will make the poultice for him. Bring me a bowl."

She mixed the linseed and oil with boiling water from the cauldron and placed it between folds of linen. Then she tested it with the back of her hand to make sure it would not burn the child. She was just placing the poultice gently upon his chest when the door was flung open and Elspeth Horne bounced in. She stood with arms akimbo on her hips.

"What's going on here, Janet Brown? What's wrong with your bairn, and what are you letting this woman do to him?" she demanded.

"He's sick——" Janet Brown began uneasily.

"Aye, I can see that for myself. What's this window doing open and all the gales of the Forth blowing in?" Elspeth Horne moved to shut it, but Barbara said in a voice of great authority, "Let the window be! I have asked for it to be opened."

Elspeth Horne scowled at her, then swerved round to Janet. "Don't you know she's done that because she thinks the boy is dying and his soul will fly out of the window and the devil will take it?"

Barbara sprang to her feet from kneeling beside the child. "That's a wicked lie! How dare you come in here making a disturbance when the child lies so ill?"

"Who has a better right? Have I not made potions for sick bairns in Culross for nigh on fifty years?" Elspeth shouted.

"Did they all get better?" James Bruce asked.

"What's that to you?" the woman snapped, rounding on him.

"I've heard of one who didn't," James said boldly. "This child's brother, William."

"Someone told you that!" Elspeth snarled, scowling at Andrew Brown. "Someone who had better watch his tongue! The lad was nigh dead when I came to him."

"Then why did you take a silver coin from Janet Brown and pretend you could cure him?" Barbara suddenly demanded in her turn.

Elspeth Horne's temper flew out of all control. "Who are you to come to Culross setting up to teach folk what to do? I tell you, my fine lady, there are queer tales going around the town, that you are not what you pretend to be."

"What do you mean?" Barbara demanded sternly, but for a moment an anxious look peered from her eyes.

"*You* should know! What's more, there are those who have seen you out at midnight, picking herbs to brew your witch's potions. Only the Horned One himself teaches you to do that."

"Be quiet and hold your silly wicked tongue!" Barbara lashed out at her.

"Witchcraft! That's what it is!" Elspeth Horne went on. She switched her attack to Janet Brown. "Will you let your bairn be treated by a witch? That brew she's given him will make him so weak that he will die, and his soul will be snatched by her master, Satan, as it soars through yon window."

Janet Brown grew pale. She knew folk said it was an ill thing to make an enemy of Elspeth Horne. In superstitious terror she half moved to the window and then stopped. Barbara's great brown eyes were upon her, beseeching.

Magdalen looked from one to the other, her hand outstretched. "Trust Mistress Barbara, Janet! Remember Elspeth Horne did not save your other child."

Elspeth gave a snort of anger and derision. "She will not save this one. I will put a spell on him."

The door was flung open and Elspeth Horne bounced in

Janet Brown gave a low moan of fear and Andrew an angry exclamation, but it was Magdalen who sprang to face Elspeth.

"Then, if this child dies, I shall go straight to my grandfather and tell him what you have said, and that *you* have bewitched the boy. Out of your own mouth you have said it, before witnesses."

It was Elspeth Horne's turn to cringe. "Nay, Mistress Magdalen, 'twas said in the heat of anger," she whined, realizing that she had said too much.

Barbara Ruthven had turned from them and was bending over the sick boy. On the skin of his forehead there was a pale glistening. "Look, James, look!" she cried. "At last it comes, the blessed sweat that will take the poisons from his blood!"

They all looked at the lad Charles. Already his breathing was easier and he had ceased to toss from side to side. Andrew Brown spoke to Elspeth Horne. "You had better go. I am content to leave my son with Mistress Barbara. I want no more of you, Elspeth Horne."

Muttering dark curses under her breath, Elspeth Horne slammed the door behind her. Barbara Ruthven looked troubled. "I fear I have made an enemy," she said.

"Aye, Elspeth is an ill woman to cross," Janet Brown replied uneasily. Through the window they could see the old woman looking back at the house, and shaking her fist.

"I'll be even with you yet, my fine lady!" she muttered.

CHAPTER 6

JAMES FULFILS HIS TRUST

CHARLES BROWN did make a good recovery, and as a result Barbara's fame as a healer was whispered through Culross and more and more quiet knocks came to her door when darkness fell. Few dared to come to her openly for fear of incurring Elspeth Horne's wrath. Whenever Barbara passed her door, the old woman's eyes followed her in dark and sinister fashion.

More and more James Bruce loved the busy life of Culross, though for him it only seemed to begin after his morning session of study with Mr. Colville. Both James and Edward were fast growing ahead of the minister's power to teach them anything new, and the way he shuffled off his duty to teach them mathematics angered Edward in particular.

"*You* could teach me more mathematics than he knows," Edward declared one day to James in careless anger, forgetting that Alexander, with his long ears, was listening and that his remark was likely to be repeated to their tutor. After that Mr. Colville looked at James with a colder, more speculating eye than ever.

"Alexander said James Bruce was kin to Lord Kinloss and had some claim on him. A pity Lord Kinloss is at the King's court in London, or we might learn the truth of this story. Whatever it is, Sir George Bruce is keeping it close enough, which bodes no good to my mind," he reasoned to himself. "And who is that strange woman the boy calls his aunt? I have seen her somewhere before, long ago, but where I cannot think. If only my memory would serve me better! And though Alexander told me her name was not really Bruce, he could not remember what her real one was."

In the afternoons James and Edward often wandered by the waterside, looking at the shipping at anchor in the bay, and listening to the many strange tongues in which the sailors spoke. Besides Sir George's fleet of coal and salt boats sailing to England and the Continent, there were ships from the Baltic ports, from Denmark, Germany, Holland, Flanders and France. They brought woollen cloth, perfume, Holland's spirits, china and tiles, and took back in turn, salt, bales of wool, barrels of salted herrings, and stacks of Culross girdles.

"What are those flat iron things like pans without sides?" James once asked his cousin, at the beginning of his stay.

Edward stared at him. "Do you mean you have never heard of Culross girdles? They're famous all over Europe. The house-wives use them for baking girdle scones and oatcakes. No kitchen is complete without one," Edward chuckled. "Come along and we'll watch the smiths making them."

There were many smithies in Culross, nigh on fifty, stretching all along the coast from Valleyfield to Dunimarle, just as almost every household had its salt-pan on the shore. All Culross rang day and night with the sound of the smiths' hammers, and the smoke from the many smithy fires and salt-pans rose above the little town towards the Abbey at the top of the hill.

The gardens and orchards and ruins of the Abbey extended right down the hill to the fringes of the town. Many of the Abbey buildings had been knocked down to provide stone for the houses of Culross after the Reformation. In the house that had once been the abbot's, next to the Abbey, Mr. Robert Colville lived.

Every Sabbath the Bruce family climbed the cobbled Tan-house brae to worship in the Abbey kirk. They had their own pews in a side chapel and Lady Bruce cast a stern eye on the younger children during the sermon, which was always very long. James Bruce and his Aunt Barbara occupied seats well to the rear of the family.

The first Sabbath, after the sermon, they had waited till the Bruce family had made a dignified exit. When the rest of the congregation filed after them, Barbara Ruthven had taken James by the arm.

"Come with me a little way. I want to show you something," she said. She led him behind the church to an iron gate set in the high wall. She opened it and beckoned him to pass through. He found himself in a beautiful garden which sloped upward to a terrace below a mansion. The front of the mansion was stately and imposing with many rows of windows.

"Why, it is a palace!" James cried.

"By rights, it belongs to you," Barbara Ruthven told him.

James went pale. "Oh, no, no, Aunt Barbara!" he cried, stepping backwards. "You cannot mean it! I—I am not worthy. What should I do with such a great place?"

"It was your father's. It should be yours, but I doubt there will be much ado to get your rights recognized in the law-courts in Edinburgh." She sounded very despondent. "Do not count on entering your inheritance for many a long year yet, though it was for this purpose I brought you to Scotland."

James Bruce looked very unhappy. "I—I would not know what to do with such a great house."

"When you are older, you will."

"Will you be there with me then?"

Barbara Ruthven shook her head. "No, James. I should do you no good. The name of Ruthven is still hated and reviled in Scotland. Once I have seen your claim to this estate go forward, I shall leave you in Sir George Bruce's care and depart from Scotland again."

"Then I shall go with you too!" James declared passionately. "I am half a Ruthven already, remember! I would rather be like you and Uncle Patrick, healing the sick, than owning this grand place and all the lands that go with it."

Barbara Ruthven suddenly turned and gathered him into her arms. "Poor laddie! You do not know what you are saying, nor what you will want some day."

"I know what I want *now*," James declared, "and it is not this."

"Maybe you will think differently later on," Barbara told him. "We had better hurry down the hill now after Lady Bruce."

In the weeks that followed, no more was said about the matter, and James fitted well into the pattern of life at Culross; the lessons with Edward; visits to the ships and the mine. He and Edward were constantly making drawings of machinery they invented for the coal-pits. In the evening James helped Lady Barbara to make medicines from the herbs she had gathered, and she instructed him in their uses for different ill-nesses. Then, too, there were always the injured children from the mine who crept to their door in the darkness for their wounds to be dressed. The days passed busily enough, and the thought of the great house at the top of the hill faded from James's thoughts, except when he and Lady Barbara made their Sabbath pilgrimage to the Abbey church.

The thought of James's claim to the house of Kinloss was always present in Barbara's thoughts, however. From the time when she had taken James as a baby, she had cherished the thought of seeing him in his father's place as a great nobleman of Scotland. It was her dearest dream. Sir George Bruce had advised her to wait and to do nothing rash in the matter, but the waiting grew tedious. Then, one day, Elspeth Horne crossed her fingers as Barbara Ruthven passed her door and cursed and mumbled at her.

"I'll know more about you yet, my fine lady! Don't think you have finished with me. A witch you are, and witches should be burnt!" She spat after her.

Barbara turned upon her. "Keep your foul tongue still, or it will be the worse for you."

Before Barbara's burning black eyes the old crone dropped her own and retired into the dark depths of her dirty cottage. Barbara knew she had an enemy, and what poison could be poured from old Bessie's tongue against her.

"The sooner I am out of Culross, the better! I must see Sir George today and ask him to put forward James's claim to his inheritance," she told herself. "When that is done, then I can go from Scotland in peace."

She waited till the afternoon when she knew that Sir George would be in his business room, and she knocked at the door. Sir George's voice bade her enter. He was seated casting up accounts when she made her curtsy to him. At once he rose and placed a chair for her.

"Your pleasure, Mistress Barbara?"

"I should be grateful for a few quiet words with you, Sir George."

"Willingly. Are you not comfortable in Bessie Barr's Lodging?"

"Oh, yes, indeed, though I feel we have been there too long."

"Oh, come now, mistress! I hear whispers of the good work you do among the children of the mine. You have done many deeds of mercy among the folk of Culross."

"If I have, I am glad of it, though it was not for that I came to Culross. Sir George, when will you be able to help James Bruce to claim what is his own before the courts of Scotland?" Barbara Ruthven put her question bluntly.

Sir George frowned and fiddled with his quill and account books. "I have already told you it is an extremely delicate business, madam. One cannot rush at it like a horse at a fence. I would like to see right done to the boy, but——"

"But you will not risk your favour with the King to do it. Is that it?"

Sir George cleared his throat. "It is not an easy thing you ask. Thomas, Lord Kinloss, is my kinsman too. You cannot expect me suddenly to thrust an unknown nephew in his place, even if *I* could do it, which is doubtful. I told you when you first came here that you would find James's claim hard to prove."

"What am I to do, then?" Barbara asked desperately. "I must have justice for the boy."

"There is one thing I might do," Sir George told her.

"What is that?"

"I might write a letter to Lord Kinloss in London and tell him of this new nephew who awaits him here at Culross. Perhaps out of his generosity he will provide for the boy."

"Provide for him?" Barbara was indignant. "But all Lord Kinloss has belongs by right to James Bruce."

"Nay, nay, my lassie, do not set your heart too high," Sir George shook his head at her. "I cannot with honesty hold out any hope to you that James Bruce will ever inherit his father's estate. There is no written record of his father's marriage to your niece Elizabeth Ruthven. His claim rests only on your word, and remember, you are a Ruthven."

Barbara's eyes grew large. "You—you mean the courts of Scotland would not take my word?"

"Just that! The King himself would oppose it."

Barbara Ruthven stared at him, then dropped her head on her arms at the table and sobbed bitterly.

Sir George looked uncomfortable, half rose, then sat down again. Like the sudden ending of a summer storm Barbara controlled her tears and forced her voice to a level tone.

"There was one other purpose for which I returned to Scotland, that James Bruce might bring the casket containing his father's heart to a fitting burial in the Abbey church of Culross. That is a sacred duty. You would not deny the boy that?"

"No, I would not deny him that," Sir George agreed slowly. "It was Edward, Lord Kinloss's right to be buried there. I will make arrangements for his heart to be placed in the Bruce chapel. But it must be done quietly. There must be no public ceremony."

Barbara lifted her eyes questioningly. As if in answer Sir George went on, "It would be necessary otherwise to get the present Lord Kinloss's consent. That would be better left till he comes home again when I can talk with him about these matters."

Barbara Ruthven bowed her head in reluctant agreement.

"Very well. I will make the necessary arrangements with Robert Colville," he promised. He passed his hand wearily across his brow.

"I—I must thank you for the kindness you have shown to me and James," Lady Barbara said. "Please do not think I am ungrateful, though I wish . . . But it is no use for a Ruthven to wish any more in Scotland," she broke off.

"You are a brave woman, Barbara Ruthven," Sir George smiled at her, but again came the weary gesture with his hand across his forehead. "I, too, am grateful for the work you have done among the poor bairns of Culross. I—I wish you could minister to me as you have done to them, my lass," he sighed.

Barbara gave him a searching glance. Though his cheeks were red it was not with the flush of health. His eyes were very heavy and tired.

"Are you ill?" she asked quickly.

"It is just these headaches, Barbara." He used her name unthinkingly, as they did in youth. "Lately they have come more often and the pain of them saps my strength. But it will go again."

"I could, perhaps, give you some medicine that would ease them," she offered. "I do not say I could cure them. That might require blood-letting by a physician."

"For that I should have to go to Perth or Edinburgh. Meantime I would be glad of your skill with herbs, my lady."

Barbara rose to go. "I will do what I can." As she turned to the door, it opened and Lady Bruce came in. Both ladies curtsied to each other coldly and Barbara went out without a word. As soon as the door was closed Lady Bruce demanded, "What was that woman doing here?"

"She came to ask a favour for the boy, something that concerns Minister Colville," Sir George told her a half-truth. "Will you send Alexander up the hill to bid him to come and speak with me, please."

"Why does she need to worry you with foolish matters about the lad's schooling?" Lady Bruce took it for granted that was why Sir George was sending for Mr. Colville. "Taking up your valuable time with her trifling business!"

"It was not altogether the lad's business we talked about," Sir George told her in fairness to Lady Barbara. "I told her of my severe headaches and asked her if she had a medicine to ease them."

"You did that?" Lady Bruce rounded upon him. "How could you be so foolish? Do you know what is whispered about her in the town? That she is a witch and collects herbs by the light of the moon, and her master, the Devil, tells her what to do with them."

"Nonsense, woman!" Sir George slapped his hand on the table. "You listen too much to the gossip from the causeways of Culross."

Lady Bruce bridled with anger. "If you drink her potions, you have only yourself to thank if any evil befalls you. I tell you, it is time that woman left Culross. She brings nothing but trouble with her."

Again Sir George wiped his hand across his eyes with a weary gesture. "Say no more, I beg you. Before long she will be gone from here."

"And high time too!" Lady Bruce declared as she stamped angrily from the room.

"Remember to send for Colville," was all Sir George said as he turned again to his accounts.

When the minister came Sir George told him as much as he thought was good for him to know. Sir George was a shrewd judge of men and he knew that Robert Colville would serve whoever held power, seeking only his own well-being. He was a lazy man, caring little for the people of his parish. With the tips of his fingers pressed together, Sir George regarded Colville over his table top.

"How is your new pupil progressing?" he asked, by way of introduction to the matter in his mind.

"Well enough, though not so quickly as Edward," Colville said, seeking to flatter Sir George in his love for his grandson.

"You think so?" Sir George gave him a shrewd glance. "Edward tells me that James Bruce is far ahead of him in mathematics."

"Ah, mathematics, maybe!" Colville answered with a sniff at the word "mathematics". "A gentleman's education is generally judged on his knowledge of the Latin and the Greek."

"I was not aware that James Bruce's education was wanting in respect of the Latin," Sir George replied drily. "From what I have seen of the lad, he has been well tutored. As for mathematics, do not despise them, Colville. For a lad like Edward mathematics will be very important. He is more likely to have to deal with problems of surveying and mining—aye, and accounts, too, than with the construing of Latin poetry. I think it might be as well if you paid a little more attention to his instruction in mathematics in future. I am not satisfied with Edward's progress there."

Colville sat in glum silence. He put this one more thing to the score against James Bruce. "I wish the lad were well out of Culross," he thought to himself.

"No doubt you have been wondering why James Bruce and his aunt have been making so long a stay here?" Sir George remarked, as though he could read Robert Colville's thoughts.

Colville started, but recovered himself quickly. "I understand they are kinsfolk on a long visit. It is not for me to wonder about the length of their stay."

"They came here for a purpose connected with our other kinsman, Edward Lord Kinloss, who died in Holland."

Robert Colville's eyes widened. He wondered what was coming next. Already, on the scanty information he had gleaned from Alexander, he had guessed at a relationship between the former Lord Kinloss and the boy. Was Sir George going to take him further into his confidence? Such knowledge might be useful when the present Lord Kinloss came again to Scotland. Under cover of the table he rubbed his hands slightly.

"As near kinsfolk, James Bruce and his aunt were entrusted with the bringing of Edward Lord Kinloss's heart back to Scotland to be buried in the Abbey church of Culross, as he wished at his death."

Robert Colville started. "But it is over twelve years since that Lord Kinloss fought his duel and died."

"Exactly! But it has not been possible to fulfil his wish and bring back his heart till now." Sir George's voice did not invite questions. "I wish now to arrange for the burial in the Bruce aisle."

Robert Colville gave him a quick glance. He remembered that James was now almost thirteen years old. "I take it, sir, that the present Lord Kinloss knows of your intention concerning his brother's heart?"

Sir George frowned. "That is a matter best talked over with him when he comes again to Culross. That may not be for a considerable time. The King's court is now in London and there is no word at all when he will next be in Scotland. For that reason I think it best to bury Edward Bruce's heart *quietly* within the Abbey church in a temporary resting place. If Lord Kinloss sees fit to have a more public funeral later, that will be for him to say."

Robert Colville bowed his head. He had learned what he wanted: that Thomas Lord Kinloss had no knowledge of James Bruce or his visit to Culross, and that Sir George had some reasons for concealing it. Could these reasons have anything to do with the lady who called herself Mistress Barbara Bruce, whose real name Alexander had said was not Bruce at all? A pity Alexander could not remember her real name!

He was brought back to attention by Sir George saying, "I will get Andrew Brown to remove one of the stones in the wall. He is trustworthy and will not noise the matter about Culross. After the casket has been placed in the wall, he will replace the stone. I will let you know which evening I decide for the burial later." His voice indicated dismissal and Colville rose to go.

A few evenings later, when most of the folk of Culross were at work around their salt-pans by the shore, a little group of people mounted the steep cobbled street past the ruins of the old monastery to the Abbey church. They were Sir George Bruce and his son George, together with his grandson Edward, and James Bruce. Beside James Bruce walked Lady Barbara Ruthven, heavily veiled. It was not the usual custom in Scotland for women to attend funerals, but she felt it was her duty to be with James at this time, and to see her sacred trust fulfilled.

In his hands James carried a small heart-shaped silver casket with a coat of arms, the cross of St. Andrew with a lion rampant in one corner of the shield, and the motto *Fuimus* on a scroll. Robert Colville was waiting for them within the porch of the church and led them silently to the Bruce aisle. There, in the shadows thrown by a flickering oil-lamp, and with a stone lying at his feet, Andrew Brown waited, mallet and chisel in hand.

Robert Colville said a prayer, then Sir George put his hand on James's shoulder. "Do your duty, lad," he whispered. James stepped forward and placed the little silver casket within the hole in the wall. He felt the terrible solemnity of the moment and hoped he was behaving with dignity, as a man might do. He stepped back and regarded the casket with reverence, though his feelings were numb, for he had never known his father. It was Barbara Ruthven who wept silently, all the springs of memory welling up within her. For a minute they all stood there as if carved in stone, then Robert Colville moved discreetly backwards and made a sign to Andrew Brown. The others withdrew quietly.

As they reached the porch the sound of the mallet was already echoing through the church. Suddenly Sir George staggered a little, then sat down abruptly on the stone bench.

"What is it, Father?" the young George Bruce asked with anxiety.

"A dizzy turn, lad. Leave me alone. It will pass."

In an instant Barbara Ruthven was at his side, pulling a tiny phial from her pocket. "Bring me a cup of water quickly," she ordered Colville.

There was a leather bottle of water and a cup for pilgrims just inside the porch and Colville seized it. Steadying her hand, Barbara Ruthven dropped three drops from the phial into the cup, shook it slightly to make the liquids mix, and then, supporting Sir George's head in the hollow of her arm, she held the cup to his lips. "Drink this," she directed.

He swallowed at her bidding and they stood watching him,

deeply concerned. It was plain this was no ordinary dizzy turn. Slowly the mists cleared from Sir George's brain, and though his head still throbbed, the church walls no longer swirled about him. He could not yet think very clearly, but he regained possession of his limbs and began to struggle to his feet, hanging on to Barbara's arm.

"Thank you, lass. I'm all right now," he muttered in a thick voice. "Thank you, Barbara Ruthven."

Indistinct as his voice was, Robert Colville caught his last words and gave a start. "Barbara Ruthven!" A quick flash of triumph crossed his face. Now he knew at last what he had wanted to know! The jumbled confusion of the knowledge he had already gleaned from Alexander fell into place like the pieces of a jigsaw puzzle. Slowly he closed his fist as if he held Sir George Bruce in the hollow of his hand. Outwardly he remained smooth and respectful.

"If you will give me your arm, sir, I will help you down the hill, with Mr. George on your other side."

Sir George muttered a half-hearted refusal, but his son welcomed Mr. Colville's suggestion. "It would be better, Father. The cobbles on the causeway are slippery with frost, and the sooner we get you home, the better."

"It would be wise to have their help down the hill," Barbara Ruthven advised him in a quiet voice. "James and Edward will run ahead and tell Lady Bruce you have not been well and ask her to prepare your bed."

"No, no! There is no need——" Sir George began, but already James and Edward were speeding on winged feet down the steep hill.

Lady Bruce was embroidering by the light of candles in the parlour when the two boys, barely pausing to knock, burst in breathlessly.

"What ails you boys? How dare you enter the room so rudely?" she exclaimed.

"Your pardon, Grandmother, but my grandfather has been taken ill," Edward gasped.

"What? Where is he?" She sprang to her feet, the reels of silk thread scattering in confusion about her.

"Father and Mr. Colville are helping him down the hill now. He is able to walk, but unsteady," Edward replied.

"My Aunt Barbara asks that you will make a bed ready for him," James told her.

The first shock of surprise wore off quickly when Lady Bruce learned that her husband was able to walk. She bridled angrily. "Your Aunt Barbara? What has she to do with it?"

"We were all at the church when Sir George was taken ill and my aunt ministered to him," James explained.

"At the church? What was Sir George doing at the church at this hour of the night? Or you boys either?" she demanded.

"We—we went there to bury my father's heart, as he had desired," James faltered.

"Your father's heart? What nonsense is this?" Lady Bruce could guess at the explanation and she was very angry.

"Please, my lady, could you make ready for Sir George? He is really sick, and perhaps tomorrow he will be better able to explain the whole matter to you than I can now," James pleaded.

Lady Bruce sent Edward scurrying from the room. "Tell Ann to put a pan of hot coals at once in Sir George's bed, and bid Bessie Horne to mix a hot posset of spiced ale and Dutch spirits for Sir George."

"I think they are coming now," James announced, looking from the window to the steps where old Henry was hurrying forward with a lantern. Lady Bruce went to the door to meet them at the top of the steps.

"Bring him in here." She indicated the parlour. "His bed will be ready in a few minutes."

Carefully they helped Sir George to the big oaken settle piled with cushions and he lay down upon it heavily.

"It's all right, my lass. Just a dizzy turn, that's all, but it's left my head throbbing."

Barbara Ruthven was not with the party. She had hurried to her own apartments and collected phials and pills in a small basket. With these she rushed back to the mansion.

George Bruce was helping his father out of his big leather boots while James took his cloak from him, as Barbara entered the room. Mr. Colville had taken Lady Bruce aside and was whispering in her ear. What he told her did not seem very welcome news, for her face grew darker and darker.

Barbara Ruthven gently closed the door behind her and

moved towards the settle, carrying her basket. Suddenly Lady Bruce barred her way, hand outstretched.

"What do you want, mistress?" she asked dangerously.

"I have brought these medicines to help Sir George," Barbara replied.

"He has no need of them. I know well enough what to give him," Lady Bruce told her.

At that moment Bessie Horne entered with the hot posset. "Here is the spiced drink, mistress," she said.

"What is in it?" Barbara Ruthven whirled round suddenly upon her.

"Why, strong ale and Dutch spirits with ginger and spices," Bessie was startled into giving an answer.

"Dutch genever?" Barbara Ruthven demanded.

"Why, yes, that is what it is sometimes called."

Barbara turned to Lady Bruce. "I beg you, Cousin, do not let him drink that posset."

"Why not? He needs warming and restoring. *I* know well enough what to give him." Lady Bruce's voice was slighting.

Barbara laid a hand on her arm. "No doubt, madam, but the posset is not the thing for a man in his condition. Besides, it would ill assort with the medicine I have already given him at the church."

"The medicine *you* have given him?" Lady Bruce's voice rose in wrath. "What witch's brew was that?"

"No witch's brew at all!" Barbara Ruthven's voice shook with cold anger. "It was a medicine to help a man as sick as Sir George is, and to fend off the blow that might fall on him."

"What do you mean?" Lady Bruce paled suddenly. "Are you ill-wishing him?"

"Indeed I am not!" This time Barbara Ruthven's anger mounted in a hot flush to her cheeks. "Listen to me, you silly woman! Your husband is very ill. Give him that posset and you may hasten his end. Give him this phial and he may live for some time longer, at least." She spoke in a rapid low tone so that Sir George could not hear.

"How do I know that? How do I know you have not poisoned him already, for you hate us all." Lady Bruce spoke with cold venom.

"That is a wicked slander! The day will come soon when you

will be sorry you have spurned my help. You are a proud woman, Margaret Bruce, yet God will blow with his wind and scatter your house of pride in ruins." There was a strange prophetic ring in Barbara Ruthven's voice. Lady Bruce shrank back from her, afraid as she had never been in all her life before. Robert Colville took a step forward, but his mouth hung open and he spoke no word. James Bruce looked from one to the other pleadingly. It was his unhappy young face that brought Barbara Ruthven back to the needs of the situation; that, and the stirring of the sick man on the settle.

"This is no time for words between us when your husband is sick. Here is the phial of medicine, Margaret Bruce, if you choose to use it. I leave him to your care." Barbara Ruthven turned abruptly and left the parlour and the door closed behind her. Margaret Bruce looked uncertainly from the phial on the table and back to her husband again.

"Which is it to be, mistress? The posset or yon thing?" Bessie Horne whispered to her, pointing to the phial.

All Lady Bruce's pride rose in her again with Barbara Ruthven's departure. "We will have the posset!" she declared, pursing her thin lips with determination. She took the pewter cup from Bessie Horne's hand and went to Sir George herself. No one saw Bessie Horne lift the phial and conceal it in the pocket of her apron. Their attention was busy with the sick man.

Once outside, Barbara Ruthven crossed the open space of the Sand Haven to the shore. The tide was coming in with a dull booming sound of waves and the drunken tilted little ships began to right themselves as the water seeped under their keels. All along the strand burned the fires of the salt-pans, tended by eerie shadowy creatures, their faces gleaming red in the glow of the flames. Their light shone upon Barbara Ruthven as she strode over the short turf. A pale moon lit a mackerel sky that looked like the reflection of the waves in the Firth, waves above and waves below. There was a thin whining whistle of wind. Barbara Ruthven paused and looked upwards with a strange foreboding, raising her hands in supplication to heaven.

It was at that moment that Elspeth Horne came to the door of her stone hut and stared across the foreshore. She clutched at the arm of her grandson, John Horne, and pointed with a skinny forefinger.

"There she goes!" she croaked. "There she goes along by the water! Look at her! Raising a wind, she is! Mark my words, lad! A witch she is, raising a wind, for sure!"

Barbara Ruthven let her hands drop to her sides and with a shiver drew her cloak about her. There was a quiet touch on her arm. It was James.

"Come home, Aunt Barbara. Come home!" he pleaded. "It is too cold out here for you." His kind young voice broke the ice in Barbara's soul.

"Oh, James!" she cried, holding him to her. "It is too cold for us both, anywhere in Scotland. Oh, the coldness of our own country to us!" She began to weep silently, bitterly. "James, James! What will be the outcome of this night's work for both of us?"

He drew her gently back towards the house near the Sand Haven. "Have courage, Aunt Barbara. You are overwrought now. The morning will make things seem better."

CHAPTER 7

THE STORM

THE next few days were full of loveliness and peace. It was near the end of March when all the warmth and beauty of spring sometimes suddenly takes the place of freezing winter. The still waters of the Firth of Forth reflected the blue of a serene sky. Beyond the Firth, in the south, the rounded slopes of the Pentland Hills stood out with crystal clearness. The warm sun beat down upon James and Edward as they stood on the stone wharf of the Sand Haven watching the loading of the salt boats. It was Wednesday, the 30th March 1625.

"A few days of this sunshine and the flourish will be out on the pear trees in the Abbey orchards," Edward remarked. The "flourish" was the old Scottish name for the sea of blossom upon the fruit trees in the spring.

Andrew Brown was standing beside them. Smiling, he shook his head at Edward. "No, lad, not yet! These are only the 'borrowing days' that winter takes sometimes from spring. Often they run before a spell of very bad weather. Those hills look too near us, indeed." He nodded his head towards the Pentlands, then looked about the skies as if searching for a sign. He found it in the small high white clouds, like the marking on a fish's back. He sniffed the air.

"Wind!" he announced. "There's wind coming, a muckle great wind!"

Edward looked where the smoke hung in thin straight columns over the red roofs of Culross. "Surely not, Andrew?" he laughed. "Why, I've never known a day so still. There's not a stir in the air nor a ripple on the water."

"It'll come for all that," Andrew declared. "This day is just a weather-breeder, mark my words! The captains of the ships would be wise to look well to their moorings and anchors."

As if he had given a signal, a sudden breeze rustled all the trees on the slopes above Culross. The willows turned their whitened under-leaves uppermost; the slender larches quivered. The very air seemed to tremble and shake for a moment and then all was still again.

"That's the beginning o' it," Andrew declared. "You'll see."

But the sun continued to shine and the waters of the Forth stayed as placid as before. James Bruce cast a glance at the coal boats bobbing up and down on the swell of the tide by the Moat Pit, and a shudder took him from head to foot, brief as the sudden wind, like a dark foreboding.

"How is your grandfather today?" Andrew asked Edward Bruce. "Is he still in his bed?"

"Do you think even my grandmother could keep him there long?" Edward laughed. "He is lying on a settle by the fire in his counting house, but he has not called for his account books, and my grandmother will not permit anyone to see him save my father."

"Aye. Word was sent to the captains of the ships that any business was to be transacted with Mr. George. Your grandfather must be sick indeed when he cannot deal with matters himself. I have never known that to happen before," Andrew said soberly.

"My grandmother looks troubled," Edward admitted. "We children have been told we are not to make any noise about the house."

"Has she asked Mistress Barbara to brew a remedy for him?" Andrew asked forthrightly.

Edward was at a loss what to reply, but James answered for him, "My aunt did leave a phial of medicine, but I do not know whether Lady Bruce made use of it."

Only Bessie Horne knew what had happened to the phial after she had slipped it into her pocket. Under cover of darkness the previous night, she had hurried down to her grandmother's house and handed Elspeth Horne the little glass phial with the silver top.

"It has Mistress Barbara's medicine inside. She wanted Lady Bruce to give it to the master, but she would not. When no one was looking, I put it in my pocket."

"What shall I do with it, then?" The old woman looked askance at the little bottle.

"Have you not been waiting the day when you could do

Mistress Barbara an ill turn? Has she not tended the sick in Culross so that they despise your potions? Though she takes nothing for doing it, yet it means less money in your pocket."

"Aye, I owe a deal of ill-wishing to Mistress Barbara," the old woman grumbled.

"Now is your chance to do more than ill-wish her! Have you still got yon poison you distilled from the Deadly Nightshade berries to kill Tom Cruikshank's mad dog?" Bessie asked.

"Aye, I still have it. But why?"

"Then empty this phial quickly and fill it again with the poison you made."

Elspeth Horne hesitated. "What do you mean to do with it?"

"Nothing that can be brought home to you. Do not fash yourself! I will take the phial back with me and wait for what opportunity brings. Haste now, and do as I told you."

The old woman emptied the phial into a bucket in the corner of the room, then she unlocked a wooden cupboard and brought out a leather bottle and dripped the contents of it slowly, drop by drop, into the phial.

"There is enough there to kill a dozen mad dogs, so mind what you do with it," she said to Bessie Horne, as she thrust the stopper back in the bottle. Bessie slipped it into her pocket and crept back to the great mansion of the Sand Haven. When she was alone in the kitchen, she lifted out a loose stone in the wall and put the phial into a small cavity behind it, then replaced the stone. "There you will stay till the time is ripe," she muttered with meaning.

Lady Bruce watched her husband with discomfort at her heart. After the hot posset he had complained that his headache was worse. "My head throbs fit to burst," he declared.

All that night he tossed in his bed, but with the first light he had risen, struggled into his clothes and made his way to the counting house, and there lay upon the settle. "I shall be cooler here," he said, but the pain did not ease.

As the day wore on he asked, "Has Barbara Ruthven nothing that will ease my headache. Oh, I know you are at daggers drawn with her, but the Ruthvens were aye skilled with herbs and potions."

"I will see what can be done," Lady Bruce said briefly. She

went in search of the phial that had been left in the parlour, but it no longer lay upon the table. After a quick hunt about the floor, she decided that Barbara Ruthven must have taken the phial away with her after all.

"Shall I demean myself to ask for it again?" she muttered proudly. "I will wait for a day. The headaches have usually eased after a day's rest. It will be the same this time, no doubt," she told herself uncertainly. "If he is no better by tomorrow, *then* I will ask for the phial back."

At sunset the sun slipped down to the horizon with an eerie orange glow shining under a dark cloud that sent its rays slant-wise upon the Firth. The grey waters seemed stained with blood. Up the Firth came great swelling rollers, black and menacing. The ships, riding at their anchors, began to swing and roll from side to side. In the east the moon rose in a queer haze that set a ghost-like ring around it. High in the sky and over the hill-tops came a peculiar whine of wind, an eldritch screeching.

Andrew Brown looked uneasily at the rising waters. "If we get the full force of a north-easterly gale behind the high spring tides, there could be damage done," he told Edward.

"Do you mean to the ships and the harbour jetty?" Edward asked.

"Aye, possibly, though I hope nought worse." His eye settled on the high wall of the Moat Pit against which the waters were churning already. "It's built right strong and it's withstood any gale that's come yet," he reassured himself.

Against the jetty wall the tide was flowing in with a peculiar smacking, sucking sound, and with each succeeding wave, the level of the water rose and fell suddenly below the wall.

"There looks to be more water than ordinar' in the Firth," Andrew Brown declared, watching the varying levels.

"Does that really happen?" James Bruce asked him.

"Aye, at the time of the spring tides I've known the marsh-lands across the water by Borrowstoneness to be flooded and all the saltings under the sea. But it's when the wind piles up the water that there's danger. Ah, weel, I'll go look to the mine draining machinery. It'll be wanted in good repair the night. It's no' high water yet by several hours."

The coal boats in the channel around the Moat Pit had to

cease their loading long before the day-workers came up the mine from their labours. The rise and fall of the tide and the breaking waves against the Moat Pit wall were too heavy to allow the coal carriers' baskets to be emptied into the hulls of the ships. Besides, no one could stand on the steps hewn into the wall without fear of being blown into the sea.

"Ye'll just have to dump the coal on the platform," Andrew Brown told them. "We'll get to work shovelling it into the boats if the wind's died down on the morn's morn."

Soon the wind was so strong that it was not safe even to step off the ladders in the well of the shaft on to the basin-like platform of the Moat Pit with the huge wall surrounding it. Even the wall could not keep back the wind which swirled round the platform. Now and again, with a heavy slap, the top of a wave fell over the wall and drained away into the runnels around the platform and back into the sea through the little gutters that pierced the walls.

Shortly after sunset the day-workers had come up the ladders at the landward exit, weary, haggard and grimy, sweating from their work down the pit, yet shivering suddenly and humping their shoulders against the savage cold wind. Usually, tired though they were, there was jesting and horseplay among the groups of young people as they went home, but not tonight. The wind took all the breath they had left. Those who turned west were blown before it like leaves. More than one small child fell to the ground and had to be helped up again by the older ones. Fighting, struggling, gasping for breath that was a pain in the chest, they battled their way across the open space of the Sand Haven with linked arms, and into the comparative shelter of the Back and Mid Causeways.

The night-workers who took their places went down the ladders with misgivings at their hearts, yet for all that, out of the force of the wind, down the mine, they felt easier.

That evening the fury of the gale put out all the fires under the salt-pans. The salt-makers retired to their stone huts and barred the doors against the still-rising storm.

In his mansion Sir George Bruce lay listening to the shrieking furies about his chimneys. It was as though the agony without matched the agony within his brain. Beside him, at his request, sat Edward, his favourite grandchild.

"Can you not sleep?" Lady Bruce asked him with pity.

"Who could? Never has there been such a wind before. I think all the time of the mine and the wall about it."

"The wall has always withstood the heaviest seas," she reassured him. "You built it good and strong."

"Aye, I built it good and strong, but this time God has sent a wind greater than man has ever known."

Lady Bruce gave a shudder. What was it Barbara Ruthven has said about the wind that should scatter her house of pride. Folk said witches could raise tempests, and Barbara Ruthven had been seen the previous night, walking along the shore lifting her arms to the skies. Bessie Horne had told her that. Sir George's voice called her back from her thoughts.

"How long is it to high tide?" he asked Edward.

"Almost an hour to go yet, Grandfather."

"Almost an hour? Till high tide is past there is no safety, no safety," he muttered to himself. As if to mock him the gale took on a yet more piercing scream. Beneath its high notes the waves crashed thunderously on the shore. The storm utterly possessed Culross.

"It is time Edward went to his bed," Lady Bruce said.

"No. Let him stay yet. With George away in Edinburgh, I have no one else to whom to turn. I might need to send a message——" Sir George's voice trailed away in weakness and suffering.

George Bruce had left for Edinburgh earlier that morning. There had been a report of one of Sir George's ships having been wrecked off Leith and George had gone to investigate.

"I hope George will be all right. The storm gets worse," Lady Bruce said uneasily. "Pray God he does not try to cross the Firth tonight!"

"He'll have more sense than to put out from Leith, but God pity those who are at sea! There will be few who could ride out such a gale."

Suddenly the whole house shuddered under a tremendous buffet of wind. There was a crash of breaking glass and a loud rattling on the roof as a chimney-pot went clattering to the ground.

"Mercy on us! I thought the house was coming about our heads," Lady Bruce exclaimed.

Sir George was sitting up in his bed. "The wall! The wall!" he cried suddenly, looking into the far corner of the room, as though he saw something they could not see. "We must get the folk out of the mine!" He gripped Edward by the arm. "Edward, are you afraid to go out in yon hurly-burly?"

Edward touched his lips with the tip of his tongue. He *was* afraid, but he would not own it.

"I will go if you wish it, Grandfather. What is it?"

"Go to Andrew Brown now and tell him to bring all the folk out of the mine at once."

"You're not wandering in your mind, are you, husband?" Lady Bruce sounded dismayed. "The folk down the mine will not be feeling the storm."

Sir George raised his voice. "In another half-hour it will be full tide and then it may be too late. Go, boy! Run! Tell Andrew not to delay." He fell back exhausted.

Edward did not hesitate. He knew well what his grandfather meant. The wall? The wall in the sea about the Moat Pit! There was a brief lull in the wind as he sped down the steps and round the corner of the house, the kind of lull when the wind only abates a few minutes, to roar again with renewed strength. It gave Edward time to get into the shelter of the gable of the great house as he ran towards Bessie Barr's Lodging.

In their little room there Barbara and James Bruce sat behind the shuttered windows listening to their incessant rattle. Now and again the house shook and black puffs of smoke came down the chimney.

"There will be no children come here tonight," Barbara said. "What are you listening for, James?"

"I thought I heard someone call—someone who shouted 'Andrew Brown'."

"Perhaps a workman from the mine?"

"No! There it is again!" James started up. "It's Edward's voice. I know it is! I must go!" He opened the door at the top of the steps and the wind tore it from his grasp and flung it back against the wall.

"I'll come with you," Barbara Ruthven cried, snatching up her cloak which billowed about her as she tried to put it on. Another second and they stood at the foot of the steps. There was Edward, hammering at Andrew Brown's door and shouting at the same time, "Andrew! Andrew! Open the door!"

As if to mock them, the gale gave a great terrifying roar and there was the sound of a chimney stack falling not far away. The wind almost plucked them from the door under the steps. Then thankfully they heard Andrew unbarring it. It was almost torn off its hinges when he opened it.

"What is it, lads? You, too, Mistress Barbara? In with you!" It took all Andrew's great strength to shut the door again.

"A message from my grandfather," Edward panted. "You're to call the folk from the mine at once, *now*, he says, before the tide is at the full flood."

Andrew stared at him. "Is it the Moat Pit wall he fears?"

"Aye!" the boy nodded.

Andrew snatched up his long coat and made for the door. "There is not much time to lose, then. Stay you here, lads!"

James Bruce, however, followed him to the door. "There isn't much time. You cannot warn them all down the mine by yourself, Andrew. There are too many tunnels. I can go along some of them for you and see everyone out."

"No, no, lad! You take your life in your hands. I'll go alone."

"We'll both come with you, Andrew," James volunteered at once.

"Yes, we'll go along the top tunnel in the mine while you take the deep one." Edward rushed to the door with him.

"Come, then, if you must. There's no time to spend arguing."

The little street of stone houses sheltered them from the worst of the blast from the sea, then they came on the open shore and the road to the mine. There was a fitful moon riding high above the racing clouds. Below it the great waves on the Firth raced with the clouds above, with a roaring din that stamped out every other sound save that of the wind. Andrew and the boys braced themselves to cross the road to the mine entrance. Even as they took a deep breath, a wave went curling over the top of the Moat Wall and broke in a thunder of inky water. Edward seized Andrew by the arm and pointed behind them. The bucket-lifting gear was motionless. The main beam of the engine was broken off. No water was being pumped from the mine. Bent double, the three of them fought their way across the road in the teeth of the gale. At last they reached the stone shelter built over the mine entrance. A voice hailed them, as another man, drenched to the skin, stumbled in after them.

"Is that you, Master Andrew? It's Tom here." Tom was the man in charge of the bucket-lifting gear. He was the one who drove the three horses round in their eternal circle. "Man, I couldna drive the horses round against yon wind. The beasts couldna face it. I was wondering what to do when the great beam came thundering down and missed me by inches. It grazed one of the horses an' the beasts took fright and burst their traces and galloped away. Where they went I cannot tell, but they disappeared into the storm as if warlocks and witches were after them."

"No time to think of that now, Tom! Come with us to get the folk out of the mine. It's not full tide yet and already the sea is pouring over the moat wall."

Andrew was half-way down the first of the mine ladders even as he spoke. The others tumbled after him. They paused only to snatch up lighted lanterns at the foot of the last flight of ladders.

"You go this way. I'll go that. Get everyone out quickly. You boys keep together," Andrew directed them briefly.

They fled along the tunnels shouting, "Out of the mine! Leave your tools and run for it! Get out at once! The sea wall may go at any minute."

No one needed a second warning. Men, women and children dropped their tools and paused only to snatch up the smallest of their bairns and heave them on their shoulders and run for the ladders. Already, as they raced along, a wave poured down the sea-entrance like a waterfall and the water began to swirl round their feet.

Madly they fought at the foot of the ladders to try to get up first, till Andrew, helped by Tom, used his strong fists to enforce order.

"The young bairns with the women first," he ordered. "I'll knock the first man down the sump who tries to get on the ladder before them."

The children needed no orders to hurry. Hand and foot, agile as monkeys they went up the ladders. At the top Barbara Ruthven was waiting to help them over the coping. She made them stand in the most sheltered part of the mine-house. "Wait there! Do not venture out into the wind till the men are

They came on the open shore and the road to the mine

here to help you across the road." The children, many of whose cuts and bruises she had tended, obeyed her at once.

Once the women and children were safely up the ladders, Andrew went back to make sure everyone was out of the mine and no one overlooked in the working-heads of the seams of coal. Tom went with him. The water was pouring down the shaft in the Firth every time a wave overtopped the Moat Wall. Already the water was swirling waist deep in the lower tunnel.

"Tom, did you see Master Edward and James go up yon ladders?" he shouted suddenly.

"N—no!" Tom faltered.

"Where, in the name o' Providence, are they? Edward! James!" he shouted, but the roar of the falling water, rushing like a torrent down the shaft, drowned his voice. With lantern held high he waded along the tunnel, peering into every miner's hole. Then Tom gave a shout, "There they are! Look where the tunnel takes a dip!" A light was bobbing erratically up and down. "God save us! James is struggling along with Master Edward on his back."

James was staggering along, the water up to his armpits, with Edward slung across his shoulder. Edward was carrying the lantern. If either of them had fallen and the light had gone out, there would have been no hope of their ever getting out of the mine again.

In a moment Tom and Andrew had waded in and seized both boys and lifted them over their shoulders. Fighting against the swirl of water about them, they reached the foot of the land-ward shaft.

"I can climb up myself, Tom," James said, struggling to his feet. "Help Andrew to get Edward up. He's twisted his foot." As they reached the top of the ladders and the land entrance to the mine, they heard the waters lapping already at the foot of the shaft.

"What happened to you, laddies?" Andrew asked, as he set down Edward.

"Thank heaven you and Tom came to look for us, Andrew! As we ran along I fell over a miner's pick and twisted my foot. I could hardly walk. I begged James to leave me and save him-self. I told him I'd try to hobble out somehow, but he wouldn't leave me," Edward told him.

"As if I would do that!" James said indignantly.

"He insisted on carrying me. But for him I might—I might have been drowned down there——" Edward faltered.

"Better get him across to my Aunt Barbara. She'll soon bind up that injured foot," James suggested.

"Your aunt has done a power of good here already tonight. She organized the folk into bands to take home the smallest children, or they'd have been blown along the road into the sea," Tom said. "And two bairns who got hurt in the rush for the ladders she took over to her own house to tend their hurts."

"There's a lull in the wind now. Make for the shelter of the cottages across the road while it lasts," Andrew said, picking up Edward to help him across the road.

They reached the steps and small stone platform with a rail outside Barbara Ruthven's door, and with one accord they paused and looked out over the stormy waters of the Forth to the wall of the Moat Pit. Already its parapet was broken and the crest of each wave rolled over it. Then, even as they looked, there came a mighty roller straight up the Firth, piling up into the narrowing funnel of the estuary, and struck the wall of the Moat Pit with a roar like an avalanche. Even above the wind they heard the sound of crumbling masonry. When the wave swept by, the wall was no more. In its place was a swirling maelstrom of angry waters.

"It's gone! Sir George's grand mine! One o' the wonders of the world! Lost under the sea for ever!" Strong man though he was, the great tears welled up in Andrew's eyes. "A sad day for Culross, this! 'Tis like to kill the master."

"Someone will have to tell him," Edward gasped. "I had better go now. Will you help me across the Sand Haven, Andrew?"

"You must have that ankle bandaged first," James Bruce insisted. "Tomorrow it might be so swollen that nothing could be done for it. Come, Edward." He drew him inside the kitchen. With skilful hands Barbara Ruthven spread a salve over the injured foot, then bandaged it firmly with clean strips of linen. Suddenly Edward began to weep.

"Does it pain you so much, laddie?" she asked him tenderly.

"No, it is not that. It is the mine—*our* mine! Oh, James, James! We had planned such grand machinery for it, you and

I. Now it will never be made. Only a few days ago I showed my grandfather some of our drawings and it seemed to make him forget his headache. He said the idea we had was good, and now—now—*I* have to tell him that the great work of his life has perished. Oh, I cannot! I cannot! And he is so ill!"

"I will go with you, Edward," James offered.

"He is still ill?" Barbara asked.

Edward nodded. "This news will go hard with him."

"Then I will come with you too, with medicines to ease the shock to him. Your grandmother will surely permit me to do that?"

A sad little procession edged its way round by the gable of the great house, Andrew assisting Edward. Henry, the watchman, was nowhere to be seen, for the great gale had driven him to seek the shelter of the kitchen.

"Do not say anything about my hurt ankle to my grandfather," Edward told them. "Already it feels much better." He opened the door and ushered them to his grandfather's room.

Lady Bruce jumped up in annoyance from her seat at the bedside. "What does this intrusion mean?" she began, but broke off when she saw their serious faces.

"We bring bad news, mistress," Andrew told her.

Sir George raised himself to a sitting position. "What is it, Andrew? What is it? You got the folk out of the mine?"

"Aye, sir, we did that; every man, woman and child."

"Thank God for that. I would not have their lives on my soul when I go to meet my Maker. But what has happened? Tell me quickly."

Andrew, tongue-tied, looked towards Edward.

"The mine, Grandfather—it's—it's——" Edward faltered.

Sir George read in the boy's face what he meant to say.

"I know, Edward, I know! When I sent you out, I was warned by a vision what might come. Is it all gone, lad? All the Moat Pit?"

Edward nodded, choking. "All under the Firth, Grandfather."

"God sent His wind and it is no more!" Sir George said, turning his face to the wall.

"God or the Devil? Which?" Lady Bruce cried. She rounded

furiously upon Barbara Ruthven. "Well, are you satisfied with what you have done, you black witch?"

Barbara stared at her, aghast. "I do not know what you mean, Lady Bruce."

"Have you come now to gloat over our misfortunes?"

"To gloat? Why should I? I came to see if I could be of help if the shock proved too much for Sir George. Should we not look to him?"

"Away with you! Do not dare to touch him! Is it not enough that you with your master the Devil raised this storm that drowned the mine?" Lady Bruce raised her hand, almost as if she meant to strike her.

"*I* raised a storm?" Barbara cried in consternation. "Oh, Margaret, Margaret! You must be demented to think it! Poor lass! Your fears for your husband, and this night's tragedy, have been too much for you. Tomorrow you'll think differently."

"Not I! I know you for what you are! A black-hearted Ruthven! All the Ruthvens have dealings with the Prince of Evil himself. Out of my house with you! You and the lad who calls himself a Bruce! He is more than half a Ruthven. Go now!"

"Grandmother!" Edward besought her. "James saved my life down the mine just now. Have pity."

"We will go. Come, James," Barbara Ruthven said with sorrowful dignity. "We shall trouble you no more, Margaret Bruce."

As the door closed behind them, the grey-faced man on the bed moaned aloud. His wife hurried to him. "What is it, husband? Are you worse?"

George Bruce could not answer her, his mouth was drawn to one side, and not a word could he speak. The stroke that had been threatening so long had fallen at last.

Andrew Brown shook his head sadly. "I doubt the loss of the mine has broken his heart."

CHAPTER 8

THE WITCH HUNT

IT WAS a grey day indeed that followed for Culross. Though the wind was less, it still blew half a gale. The miners gathered on the shore and looked at the place where the stout wall of the Moat Pit had risen triumphantly above the waves. Its great stones were scattered far and wide over the muddy banks of the Firth when the tide went down. Where the pit shaft was, the tide rushed in with a whirling motion and a curious sucking sound. The men looked at each other with grim faces.

"There'll be no more coal hewn out o' yon pit," one man declared, "No coal! No wages! No bread! There'll be bairns crying o' hunger soon."

Andrew Brown returned from inspecting the landward entrance to the mine. He ventured a few feet down the ladder only to find water lifting and falling in the shaft with the movement of the tide.

"Any hope o' draining the water off, Andra?" one of the men asked him.

He shook his head. "No, lads. I'm thinking the sea has ta'en the mine for good. We couldna lift out all yon weight o' water before the tide will have filled it again."

"Will Sir George open up another mine, think you?"

"Sir George lies grievously ill, lads, at death's door. The news about the mine was too much for him."

This was shocking news indeed for all of them who had great respect for the "old master" who provided them with their living.

"But surely young Master George will find work for us?" one of the men said.

"That I cannot tell you, lad. He has not returned from Edinburgh yet, and can't, till the wind drops more still. A sorry state of affairs he'll find at Culross, for we're not the only one to suffer at the mine." Andrew Brown gestured towards the Firth.

The shores were strewn with the wrecks of ships, their wooden hulls battered and broken, their masts lying over the sides in a tangle of ropes. Many of their crews had been sleeping aboard and had tried to up-anchor and bring their ships into the shelter of the harbour when the storm had increased in fury. Nearly all had perished with their ships, and their pitiful bodies were cast up by the tide along the muddy foreshore.

Most of the inhabitants of Culross were out looking at the ruins of their salt-pans; the big boilers overturned by the waves, the fires all out and the ground sodden beneath them.

"It'll be more than a week afore we can set all this to rights again. And even when we do get the salt-pans boiling, where are the ships to take our salt to England? Half the salt fleet is under the sea," one salt-maker cried.

"The like of this tempest was never seen in our time, nor any before it," a sailor's wife wept.

Mr. Colville was down on the shore shaking his head over the ruins of his congregation's works.

"Aye, there was never a storm like this within the memory of man," he agreed. "Such a tempest aye bodes some great evil. It'll be the forerunner of something terrible yet to come."

Mr. Colville never hesitated to predict the most gloomy events to his flock, but almost as if to prove his premonitions true, a horseman came galloping into the town along the road from Stirling. He drew up at the entrance to Sir George Bruce's house and threw the reins of his horse to one of the crowd.

"News! News!" he shouted. "I have news for Sir George Bruce."

Edward Bruce had been watching the milling crowds along the shore and at the Sand Haven, and looking anxiously across the Firth for any sign of his father's ship from Leith. When he saw the horseman on his lathered horse, he ran down the steps to meet him.

"Sir George Bruce? I must see him." The messenger sounded very important.

Edward held him by the sleeve. "If you please, sir, tell your news to me. I am grandson to Sir George Bruce. My grandfather is too ill of a stroke even to understand what you are saying."

"Your father, then? Mr. George Bruce? Where is he?"

"He is in Edinburgh transacting business for my grandfather. His return by ship from Leith has been delayed by the storm. If you will give me your message I will see it is told him as soon as he arrives."

"If he is in Edinburgh he will have heard the news already. It is the blackest news that has been brought to Scotland this many a day. The King is dead!"

A shudder of horror shook the crowd.

"What did I tell you?" Robert Colville cried in a voice almost of triumph. "I said the storm boded worse to come! When did His Majesty die?"

"On the Lord's Day, about noon, five days ago in London, when you were all at your prayers." The messenger had a keen sense of his dramatic news. "The tidings reached Stirling from Edinburgh only this morn and I travelled at once to bring the unhappy news to Sir George and the other noblemen of Fife. King James is dead! Long live King Charles!"

"It is a sad loss, a grievous loss to Scotland indeed!" Mr. Colville made his voice heard. "King Jamie the Sixth of Scotland and First of England is gone! May the Lord have mercy on him."

"Bad news aye comes on wings. You'd think Mr. Colville enjoyed it, the old crow!" Magdalen whispered to James, who with his Aunt Barbara, had come from their lodging to find out why the crowds were gathering about the solitary horseman. "Here comes my grandmother now to hear the tidings."

Lady Bruce came down the steps into the forecourt, and Edward went towards her to break the news quietly to her, but Mr. Colville forestalled him.

"Sorrow upon sorrow, my lady! After the tempest, wrecked ships, drowned men, ruined homes and now the worst of all, the tidings of death!" he exclaimed, turning each phrase on his tongue with relish.

Lady Bruce turned pale, put her hand to her heart, and almost fell. "Not George! Not my son! Oh, no!" she whispered in horror.

While pleased at the dramatic effect of his news, Mr. Colville hastened to reassure her, "No, no, my lady! Not Mr. George! 'Tis the King himself. King James is dead."

The colour began to come back in Lady Bruce's face, but she schooled herself not to express relief that the news was not about her own family. "These are sorry tidings indeed. I dare not tell Sir George. Coming as it does on all Culross has suffered from the storm, it would be the death of him too. It is not long since His Majesty was our welcome guest here at Culross." She shook her head sadly.

"Sir George was aye a loyal subject to His Majesty," the messenger said. "And now, by your leave, my lady, I'll be on my way to Dunfermline."

Lady Bruce knew what was expected of her. She took a golden coin from the purse that dangled from her waist and gave it to the messenger. "See that the rider gets a mug of ale, Henry," she ordered the gaping watchman.

"Woe upon woe! Woe upon woe!" Mr. Colville chanted, moving among the people. "Disaster on disaster!"

"There's one who doesn't think it!" came a woman's voice from the crowd. "Look at the one there who calls herself Mistress Barbara Bruce. There's no sorrow in *her* face." Elspeth Horne pointed to Lady Barbara, standing with James and Magdalen, a little apart from the crowd.

In truth, Barbara Ruthven's face held a kind of relief. The news the messenger had brought meant that the lifelong enemy of her family was dead; that she and her brothers need go no longer in fear of imprisonment and death; that there was hope at last that James Bruce's claim might have a chance of being heard in the law courts of Scotland. Her honesty would not let her pretend a sorrow she did not feel, and despite Elspeth Horne's pointing finger, she refused to draw a mask of mourning over her face.

"Look at her! Look at her!" Elspeth Horne shrieked. "Can ye doubt but that she ill-wished the King himself, as she did Sir George and the Moat Pit o' Culross?"

There was a stir of excitement ran through the crowd. Most of them were filled with the superstitions of the age and believed in witches and their evil powers. Even the King himself had ordered witches to be tried.

"I have ill-wished no one," Barbara Ruthven said with dignity.

"*She* has brought these evils on Culross. I saw her the night before the storm, walking along the beach at sunset with her arms outstretched, calling down the tempest upon us. She cannot deny it!" Elspeth Horne declared.

"It is true I walked on the beach. There is nothing wrong in that. But it is not true that I called up the storm. Only God can blow with His wind," Barbara replied.

"Aye, but the Devil too can send a wind of destruction when a witch like you calls on him to do it," Elspeth shouted. "A witch she is, I tell you all!"

"She's a witch! She's a witch!" It began to be murmured among the folk. They looked shiftily at Lady Barbara and there was an ugly surge of the crowd towards her. She stood her ground and stretched out her hands towards them.

"Have I not lived here in quietness, trying to do works of healing among you?" she appealed to them.

The crowd halted. There were many among them miners whose children she had tended.

"Aye, folk, that's true enough," Andrew Brown stood up for her. "She healed my own child when he was like to die of a fever of the lungs."

"She did it by witchcraft," Elspeth Horne yelled. "She bewitched ye, Andrew Brown, even as she bewitched Sir George himself and caused him to lose his speech and brought him close to death."

"That's a wicked lie!" Barbara declared hotly. "You know it is untrue, Lady Bruce. You know that I did all I could to help your husband, aye, and would have done more, if you would have let me. Will you not speak for me?"

Lady Bruce looked at her coldly and did not speak.

"Aye, true it is you would have done more!" Elspeth Horne jeered. "Bessie!" she shouted to her daughter who had appeared behind Lady Bruce on the steps of the mansion. "Tell the folk about yon phial that Mistress Barbara left behind her to be given to Sir George."

Bessie looked triumphantly to Lady Barbara. "*I* took the phial into my keeping."

"Why did you do that?" Lady Bruce asked quickly. "I looked for it, hoping it would relieve my husband's suffering, but it was not to be found."

"Aye, if would have relieved his suffering right enough, your ladyship," Bessie said grimly. "It would have brought death to him."

"Oh, no, never!" Barbara declared.

"My aunt would never do such a thing! She is no murderer," James cried boldly, though he was white-faced. He stood before his aunt as though to defend her.

"That phial held poison!" Bessie Horne told them. "I proved it!"

Mr. Colville thought it was time his voice was heard, though his face held no pity for Lady Barbara.

"How did you prove it, Bessie Horne?"

"Ask old Henry here," Bessie said, in a voice of triumph. "He'll tell you."

"Bessie Horne told me she had found the phial but that she mistrusted what was in it. She swore it held a poison," Henry croaked in his old quavering voice. "She said she'd test it, and she poured it into the milk the cat was lapping up."

"And what happened?" Mr. Colville demanded.

"The cat lapped it up, then reeled and rolled over dead. I saw it with my own eyes."

"The cat's here, under the steps," Bessie Horne cried. "I kept it as proof." She lifted out the poor pitiful body and held it up. A wave of horror and indignation swept the crowd.

Barbara held out her hands towards Lady Bruce. "That was not my medicine!" she cried. "I swear my physic would not bring death to any creature. I beg you to believe me."

Lady Bruce turned a stony countenance upon her. "You are a Ruthven. All the Ruthvens have knowledge of the Black Arts and are in league with the Devil. You would have poisoned my husband."

"No, no! As God is my judge, I swear it is not true," Barbara cried, the tears streaming down her face.

"She's a witch—a witch—a witch——!" The murmur grew louder in the crowd. The thought of all the disasters and distress the storm had brought upon them incensed them more. "Try her for a witch! Throw her in the sea! If she swims, then she is a witch!" one man cried.

"Prick her with your knives to see if she bleeds. She has brought sorrow and hunger and death to Culross," Elspeth Horne shrieked.

There was an ugly movement among the crowds towards Lady Barbara and James.

"Duck the lad too. He's another of the same breed!" John Horne added his voice. He rushed up to lay his dirty hands on James. This was more than Edward Bruce could stand. He stepped forward bravely, but with a pale face and working lips, before Lady Barbara and James Bruce.

"Touch them at your peril, you filthy lout!" he shouted at John Horne. "I'll have you know that this lad is a Bruce and kin to us. While my grandfather is sick and my father is not here, then *I* speak for the Bruces. Let not one of you dare to lay a finger on them!" His clear ringing voice stopped the mob in its first mad rush towards Barbara. Even John Horne fell back a pace or two.

Elspeth Horne was not defeated, however. She knew she had the silent support of Lady Bruce.

"But the woman is not a Bruce," she declared. "Yon witch is a Ruthven. Her ladyship herself has said it."

"Nevertheless, she is under my grandfather's protection," Edward asserted boldly, daring his grandmother's anger.

"Did not the King himself say the Ruthvens were to be destroyed root and branch, that their name should be no more spoken in Scotland," Elspeth Horne demanded. "And the King not cold in his grave! Would you forget that?"

This was a cunning appeal to their loyalty that it was not likely the crowd would withstand. Two men seized Barbara Ruthven by her arms and twisted them behind her back. James struck at them and pulled and tugged to free her.

Robert Colville decided matters were getting out of hand and it was time for him to assert his authority. Besides, something Elspeth Horne had said sent a quiver of foreboding up his spine. The King *was* dead. The enemy of the Ruthvens was in his grave and who knew what strange swing of fortune might make the lad James Bruce lord of the mansion behind the church? Colville's living might then rest in his hands. Besides that, George Bruce's wife, Mary Preston, was said to be a friend of Lady Barbara's. What might George Bruce say on his return if he found violence had been done to Barbara Ruthven and he, Robert Colville, had looked on and said nothing? Robert Colville liked to have a foot in both camps.

Just as the crowd surged round and began to hustle Barbara Ruthven towards the sea, he sprang on a mounting block and shouted to them, "Wait, good people! Hear first what I have to say!"

Accustomed to obeying their minister, the mob halted, angered and inflamed though they were.

"Would you not be better to wait for Mr. George to return from Leith before you put the witch to her trial?" he asked.

"Why should we wait?" John Horne cried impudently. "Has she no' been proved to be a witch? Burn her, I say! Build a fire round her feet and see if her master the De'il will fly awa' wi' her."

"Aye, what does it say in the Good Book, Minister? It says, 'Thou shalt not suffer a witch to live!' " Elspeth Horne reminded Robert Colville with triumph.

"True, old woman," he said smoothly. "But not all witches have been brought to their trial, even in Culross."

This prod reminded Elspeth Horne that she had taken money secretly for spells and love potions from many of the folk in the crowd. It would not take much in their present excitement for them to turn on her too. Indeed, Isobel Norrie's mother swung round and jeered at her. "What's wrong wi' putting two witches on their trial?" she demanded.

"One at a time, folk, one at a time!" Robert Colville urged. "But let all be done according to the law. It would not do for you to take the law into your own hands, and then be brought to book for it yourself, afterwards."

The crowd hesitated. Robert Colville went on, "Is it not the law that witches should be tried in Edinburgh and burned on the esplanade of the castle there?"

Lady Barbara Ruthven moaned and shut her eyes. What chance would she, a Ruthven, have before a grim-faced Council in the law courts of Edinburgh? Better let death come swiftly now in the grey waters of the Forth, than slowly in a cat-and-mouse game of a trial ending in a burning on the high hill of Edinburgh.

"Throw me in the sea, if you must. My death will prove my innocence," she cried.

"No, no! That is too good for a witch who is a poisoner," Bessie Horne cried. "Let justice be done here in Culross. Light the fire now, I say!"

"Stay your hands!" Robert Colville thundered. "What you do in hot blood today cannot be undone tomorrow, when George Bruce returns home. And if it is as the lad Edward Bruce says, that she is under the protection of the Bruces, how will you answer for it to George Bruce? Remember he is your master and you are his servants and that many of you will lack work tomorrow, and be beseeching the young master to find it for you."

The timely reminder warned many of the hot-heads that their bread depended upon George Bruce. Some of the women-folk tugged at their husbands' sleeves and whispered, "They say the young Mistress Bruce is a friend to yon woman."

"How then? Should we suffer a witch to go free?" a surly salt-panner cried. "Think of the havoc she wrought on Culross last night!"

"It was not my doing, good folk. The storm was not of my making," Barbara Ruthven besought them to believe her.

"All that will be proved at the trial," Colville assured them smoothly. "No doubt the trial can be arranged to take place here at Culross, when Mr. George returns." He knew the mob would want their sport out of a witch. "Have no fear! She will not go free. I ask you but to wait till tomorrow till Mr. George comes home, and then everything shall be done according to the law and no man will be called on to answer for the part he has played in a burning."

"The minister is right! Wait till the young master comes home," Andrew Brown urged them, hoping to save Barbara Ruthven from their cruel violence.

"Tomorrow the witch will provide as much sport as today. Let us build up our salt-pans again today, and start the fires going under them, then we can carry her from pan to pan and toast her toes at each one tomorrow and make her confess her evil deeds," a cruel-looking man suggested.

"Aye, do that! Just that!" Elspeth Horne clapped her hands.

James Bruce clung to his aunt's arm. "Don't faint, Aunt Barbara," he whispered to her. "They'd never dare." But he was not sure of it in his own heart. He knew well the cruel ways men used to torment witches to obtain demented "confessions", the fire and the pincers and the rack.

"What's to be done with her, then?" a bold woman cried.

"Fling her in the jail!" a man suggested.

"The jail is ower full of evil-doers already. Better deal with her now," John Horne's father Adam Horne declared.

"No. We will not risk putting her in the jail. The Devil might pluck her out of it. No, we will put her in a place where her spells will have no power and where the Devil cannot come," Robert Colville told them. "We will put her where witches have been kept before—in the tower of the Abbey kirk."

"Aye, aye! That's the place. Carry her to the kirk tower!" the crowd shouted. "Up the hill to the tower wi' her!"

Jostling and pushing, the mob dragged Barbara Ruthven up the hill.

"Mercy! Have mercy!" she cried, as they punched and pulled at her. Elspeth Horne spat upon her and pinched her. Once Barbara sank to her knees on the cobbled causeway, half-fainting, but a jerk at her arms by Elspeth's son Adam brought her staggering to her feet again. James tried to range himself alongside her and shield her with his own body, but he was roughly thrust aside and fell in the gutter at the side of the causeway. Someone gave him a hand to pull him to his feet. It was Isobel Norrie.

"Take courage, Master James!" she whispered in his ear.

"What will they do to her? What will they do to her?" he cried desperately. He found Edward and Magdalen were beside him.

"If she is imprisoned in the tower she will be safe at least from their wicked hands," Magdalen said.

"But only till tomorrow. What is to stop them dragging her out then and burning her?" The tears rolled from James's eyes in the torment of his heart.

"Do not despair! All is not lost. There is maybe a thing can be done yet," Isobel Norrie told him with meaning in her voice.

"Oh, why did we ever come here?" he cried unhappily. "It was for my sake she came back to Scotland. I wish we had never left Holland."

"Holland?" Isobel Norrie said. "Maybe, even yet——" Her words were lost in the shout of the crowd as they reached the doorway of the Abbey church.

They flung back the great door with violence and as many as could pushed and jostled to get inside the square porch with their prisoner. The door to the tower stairs lay to the left, a little apart. They kicked it open.

"Have a care, good folk! Do no damage to the property of the church," Mr. Colville besought them, standing on the tower steps to make himself heard. He was almost overwhelmed by the rush up the stairs. Dragged upwards with her knees knocking against every stair, bleeding and scratched, Barbara Ruthven was flung on the wooden floor of the topmost room. The breath was knocked out of her body and she lay there unconscious.

"We'd better bind her, in case she flies through yon window," Adam Horne said, pointing to a small circular opening in the stonework, high in the wall.

"Use the bell rope to bind her, Father," John Horne suggested.

Knives were brought out and a length of the bell rope was hacked off.

"Why not hang her from the top of the roof while you're about it and let her dangle over the tower?" a man shouted.

"Hanging's too good for such a one!" Elspeth Horne declared. "Wait till you've got your fires going under the saltpads and we'll have our sport with her first."

Colville began to be afraid the mob would get out of hand. "Aye, go home, good folk. There's nothing more to be done now. The woman has lost her senses and cannot heed what you say or do to her."

"Aye, no cat plays wi' a dead mouse," another man said coarsely. "Leave her to come to! She canna stir wi' yon rope bound round her."

"Who'll see she's locked in?" Adam Horne asked.

"I have the key to the tower. If you'll all step down the stairs, *I'll* lock it and keep the key myself," the minister promised them. He shoo'd them out before him like a flock of geese, then, when he had them all in the porch, he sighed with relief and locked the door to the stairs.

"You're sure no one can get in to let her out?" Adam Horne said. "What about the door into the porch?"

"Set a guard in the porch if it pleases you," Colville said with some impatience. "Maybe your lad and another would serve?"

"Up the hill to the tower wi' her!"

John Horne drew back, grumbling. "It would be right cold sitting there a' night on a cold stone bench. I dinna fancy it alone."

"Maybe Thomas Bowman will keep you company?" The minister pointed to a young man of about eighteen. "I'll see you get two comfortable chairs from my house and your supper with a mug of well-spiced ale. And there'll be a penny for you in the morning." A penny in 1625 was worth quite as much as two shillings now. Robert Colville was anxious to get the mob away before any damage was done to his church, for which he might have to answer to Lord Kinloss.

"Then we'll keep guard," Thomas Bowman agreed.

They did not see Isobel Norrie among the crowd, nor the gleam that came into her eye at the mention of the spiced ale.

The crowd clattered away noisily down the hill, and the minister departed with relief to his manse, but wondering with some anxiety what the next day would bring.

CHAPTER 9

THE KEY

ISOBEL NORRIE hung behind the rest of the crowd till they reached the Market Cross in the tiny cobbled square where the roads divided. Ahead of her, lower down the hill, she could see James walking between Magdalen and Edward. They took the turning towards the Sand Haven mansion. Quick as a cat Isobel skirted the crowd and darted along a narrow wynd with a high cobbled crown, past two or three cottages, and reached the place where the lane narrowed to a track that ran along the verge of the cliff-like rocks that overhung Culross. It was a steep slippery path but Isobel was as sure-footed as a goat. She ran along the edge of the great wall that buttressed the cliffs, till she reached a path like a gully that ran at right angles between high walls by the side of Sir George Bruce's garden. It descended to the Sand Haven by a long flight of steps, moss grown and crumbling. The steps came down by the side of Bessie Barr's Lodging.

Isobel guessed that the children would make for this place with James and stay to comfort him. She leaped down the steps to get there before they did. She did not want anyone in the crowd to see her. When she reached Bessie Barr's cottage there was no one in sight. From the noise she guessed the folk were still at the far side of the Sand Haven. Quietly as a mouse she scuttled up and lifted the latchet of the door. She had guessed right. It was not locked. Barbara Ruthven and James Bruce had left it in too great a hurry when the messenger arrived. She crept inside and waited, blowing on the dying embers of the fire. James would be cold from fear as well as from the bitter wind. She thought of Barbara Ruthven lying bound on the cold floor of the icy church tower and sobbed with pity for her. It was only a matter of moments before she heard the steps of the other three children on the stone stair outside. They came in silently, unhappily, like fugitives, and Edward slipped the bar across the door. It was only when they turned to the fire that they saw Isobel standing in the shadowy inglenook.

"You here, Isobel?" Magdalen said with surprise.

"Yes, I am here to do what I can. It was because of her compassion for me that Mistress Barbara was put out of the great house by Lady Bruce. It was I who brought other bairns to be healed, and that made Elspeth Horne hate Mistress Barbara. It is all my fault." Her tears fell.

"Isobel, it would have happened if any child had come to her, not just you. There was never a Ruthven yet who could turn aside from the mysteries of healing." James spoke with an inner knowledge that was strange in so young a lad. "But what's to happen to her tomorrow?"

"Surely my father will be home by tomorrow——" Edward began.

"But if father is delayed, what will happen then? The folk will not be denied their sport for long." Magdalen spoke bitterly.

"Aunt Barbara could die of cold in that terrible tower," James moaned. "Oh, if only I were with her! Why did I not manage to keep alongside her, then they would have imprisoned me too."

"I know a thing——" Isobel Norrie began, then stopped. "But it might mean danger for James, for all of you. I am not sure it could be done."

"Tell us, for the love of heaven," Magdalen said. "Is it something that would help Mistress Barbara?"

"I know a secret way into the church," Isobel told them.

They froze at once to attention, looking at her with wide eyes.

"You know my family were once gipsies? We were not always miners. In the summer we used to roam the Highlands, but when the winter came we always made for Culross, and my father used to get a kind of living, helping the shoremen to work the boats alongside the ships to bring in the cargo. He used to build a rough kind of stone shack for us on the hill just below the church, out of the many old stones that lie there."

"Yes, those stones were once part of the great monastery that was at Culross a hundred years ago," Edward explained.

"Aye, we knew they belonged to the buildings of the old monks. Not many of the folk of Culross disturbed us there, for they believed the place was haunted. The year before we all went to work in the mines, we were staying in the old stone hut he had made from the ruins. I was left to tend the fire while he and my mother went to see what they could beg from the sailors when the ships came in. I got weary in the hut by myself and I began to wander about on the hill."

"Go on!" Magdalen urged her, leaning forward eagerly in the firelight.

"There was a hole behind an old stone pillar, and I thought a fox or rabbits might be in it. I put my arm down and found that it widened out inside, and I thought I could see stones built into a wall under the ground. I went back to the fire and lighted a dry branch, then returned to the hole. When I looked inside, I saw it was the entrance to a stone passage."

"Did you go along it?" Edward asked tensely.

"I scraped away the earth from the entrance a bit more first, got another lighted branch and went a few yards along the passage. The tunnel mounted by some steps, then there was a slanting passage. I did not dare go far, for the branch might burn itself out before I got back and I was afraid to be left in the dark."

"How did you know the passage ended in the church, then?" Edward asked.

"I bided my time for a few days until my father and mother went begging round the farms. As soon as my parents were out of sight I found the old lantern my father uses when he is poaching salmon, or helping the smugglers land their French brandy. There was plenty of oil in it. I lit it with a faggot from the fire and went to explore the passage. The long slope of the tunnel ended in a few more steps that came to a sudden end at a stone wall built across it. I was vexed to find it finished like that, for every bairn thinks of treasure. I cast the light from the lantern around and then I saw the stone slab just above my head. There were two steps in the wall that seemed to lead up to it. Something made me put the lantern down and push at the stone with my hands. At first nothing happened, then it seemed to move just a little and to tilt, so that one edge of it seemed lower than the opposite one. I pressed harder on one side and it swung back on a pivot."

The children held their breath.

"At first I was afraid to go farther," Isobel confessed.

"But you *did* go on?" Edward questioned her.

"Yes, I did. I managed to reach up and put the lantern in a niche that seemed made for it, just inside the hole, then I found there were tiny steps cut in the wall by which I could pull myself up. I reached for the lantern and held it high. It was then

I found I was inside the church, in the part belonging to your family today, the part you call the Bruce chapel. Yon slab was one of the paving stones."

"The tunnel must have been a secret way out of the church to the monastery building," Edward exclaimed.

"Or a secret way *into* the church!" Magdalen cried with meaning. "Where the monks once went, we can go too. We can get inside the church to Mistress Barbara."

"Yes, but remember the door to the tower is locked and Mr. Colville holds the key. Even if we get in the church, how can we reach her?" Edward pointed out.

"There are two guards placed in the church porch too; John Horne and Thomas Bowman. We have to go through the porch to get to the tower." James shook his head despondently.

"There might be a way to get rid of *them*."

"How?"

"Mr. Colville promised to send a mug of spiced ale to them. Perhaps *we* could take up the hot spiced ale?"

The other three looked at Isobel in surprise.

"Has your aunt no medicine that will send people to sleep?" Isobel asked James pointedly.

"I understand. Why, yes! When Andrew Brown's bairn was so sick; he was restless and she made up a physic that would give him sleep. Now, let me see, which was it?" James jumped up and began to rummage among the bottles in the cupboard that contained his aunt's medicines. "Here it is! An infusion made of box leaves and a powder my aunt got in Italy."

"It is not a poison?" Isobel asked anxiously.

"My aunt would never use a poison," he assured her. "Whatever Bessie Horne gave to that cat, it was not my aunt's physic."

"I do not trust Bessie Horne. She is a sly scheming woman," Magdalen declared. "If my grandmother could see farther than the end of her nose, she would soon find that out." She turned to Isobel. "What do you want with the sleeping potion, Isobel? I think I can guess. Is it for the spiced ale?"

Isobel chuckled. "Yes, if the ale is spiced highly enough, those two brutes in the church porch will never taste the sleeping potion in it. But it will have to be carried to them when it is dark."

"The minister would likely send it by Alison, his maid-servant. She has a high mincing voice. I could imitate her easily," Magdalen declared. "I will carry up the ale. All I need to do is to set it down on the step, bang on the church door and cry, 'The meenister has sent you your ale. It is on the step,' and hurry away. By the time they have unbarred the door I shall be past Mr. Colville's gate and round the bend of the wall. They'll never see me."

"That's well thought out!" Isobel clapped her hands. "By the time we go up the tunnel into the church, they'll both be sound asleep and snoring hard."

"But what is the use of getting into the church if we cannot unlock the door to the tower?" James asked. "Until we can do that, there is no hope of escape for her."

"Maybe we could break the lock?" Isobel suggested. "I could get my father's pickaxe."

Edward shook his head. "Think how the blows would echo in the tower and all over the hill-side. There are people in cottages near by and they would surely hear. We might even rouse the sleepers in the porch or the minister himself. We have still to get Mistress Barbara out when we have opened the door, you know."

"And we cannot tell how ill or injured my aunt might be after the way she was treated yesterday. We might have to carry her down those steps," James pointed out.

" 'Tis plain whatever we do must be done quietly. The minister holds the key. We must get it from him in some fashion," Magdalen declared, chewing the tips of her fingers. "But how? Will the minister carry it in his pocket, do you think?"

Edward shook his head. "It is far too big and clumsy. It must weigh nearly a couple of pounds. He would never put that in the skirts of his coat."

"Where then, would he keep it?"

"Most like in his parlour, in his big desk. It has drawers."

"Do the drawers lock?" Magdalen asked.

"That I cannot remember," Edward told her. "We must take a chance on it. I will go and see him and tell him I am very concerned about Mistress Barbara and implore his pity and his help for her until my father comes home. I must try and make an opportunity to be in the room alone and to search for the key."

"Listen, Edward!" Magdalen said, her eyes alight. "The best chance will be for you to go when the minister has his supper. That is at half-past seven. It would be best for you to go to see him a few minutes after that, just when he has begun to eat. If I know Mr. Colville he will not leave his broth to go cold while he talks with you. He will let you wait until he has finished his meal, and you know Alison generally shows visitors into his parlour."

"You're right!" Edward exclaimed. "That might be my chance to find the key. I'll do it!"

"Then we will prepare the spiced ale and be ready to heat it if Edward comes back with the key. It will be dark by then," Magdalen said. "The sun is setting already."

"What about your own supper?" James asked. "Will not Lady Bruce ask where you are if you are not at the table?"

Magdalen shook her head. "Since my grandfather was so ill she has taken all her meals in his room. She will not leave him. We children are not allowed to go near him, for he cannot stand any noise." Magdalen's eyes misted with tears.

"But your mother? Will she not wonder where you are?"

"I will go to her now and ask if Edward and I may stay for a time this evening to comfort you, James. It is what she would expect us to do. She is fond of your aunt, too."

Magdalen scampered away and soon returned bringing a large pewter jug of hot broth with meat in it. "Mother is busy with the baby. She told me to bring this for our supper, Edward. Get out the bowls and spoons and we will all share it."

James at first seemed little inclined to eat, but Magdalen urged him, saying, "You may have need of all your strength before this night is out."

By the time they had finished their meal it was dark, and Edward set off on his journey up the hill to the minister. Though his ankle was still sore and he limped a little, it was much easier for Lady Barbara's treatment, and he could walk without much difficulty.

"Bar the door after me," he said. "I will tap three times when I return, so you will know who it is. I will go up by the Little Wynd. I am less likely to meet anyone there than on the Causeways. Most of the folk are down on the shore repairing the gear of their salt-pans."

Keeping to the shadows thrown by the cottages, Edward hurried soft-footed up the hill. There, high walls lined the road and there were no more houses, only the ruins of the monastery. He reached the crown of the hill and the minister's house just below the Abbey church. He took a deep breath, opened the gate and strode up to the door. He tirled the ring up and down the corkscrew iron by the door, and it echoed over the hill with a loud ringing sound. A minute went by, then the door was opened by a neat maidservant, holding a lantern high, the better to see who was at the door.

"I wish to speak to Mr. Colville," Edward said.

The girl hesitated. "He—he is at his supper, young man."

"I am Edward Bruce," Edward told her quietly. "Do you think I could wait to speak with him? My business is urgent."

At the mention of his name she ducked a bobbing respectful curtsy. "La, Master Edward, I did not know you with your collar pulled up about your ears."

" 'Tis cold, Mistress Alison," Edward replied.

"Come in, sir." She led the way to Robert Colville's parlour. "Sit you by the fire while I acquaint the minister that you are here. But—but he is at his meat, you know."

"Tell him I will wait," Edward said, taking a seat by the fire while she lighted a taper at it and put it to each of the candles in the sconces on the table and mantelpiece. Hardly was she out of the room than he snatched up a candle and rushed to the minister's desk, and looked hurriedly through the drawers. They contained nothing but the minister's papers, no solid object at all like a key. Edward was about to give up the search when he noticed that the top drawer which he was putting back in the desk seemed shorter than the others he had pulled out. Hurriedly he compared it with the drawer below. It *was* shorter! That meant there must be a space behind it. He put in his hand and felt in the space at the back of the drawer compartment. Something cold and hard was there! Hardly daring to hope, he pulled it out. It was a large iron key!

Quick as thought he pushed the drawer into place again. The key was too large to go into his pocket without it showing. Where to hide it? Already he could hear the door opening from the dining-room into the passage and Mr. Colville's step on the stone floor. Of a sudden inspiration came to him! He thrust it into the lining of his high-crowned hat. By the time the minister opened the door of the study, Edward was sitting sedately on a chair by the fire, with his hat resting on his knees. He rose respectfully when Mr. Colville entered the room, taking care to hold his hat by the brim and keep it upside down in his hand.

"Well, Edward, this is a somewhat inconvenient time to seek me out," he said in a cold voice. "I was at my supper."

"Your pardon, sir. I would not have troubled you now, but concern for Mistress Barbara brought me here."

"Is that not a matter better left for your elders?"

"Sir, my grandfather lies very ill and my father is away from home. At this time I am the only one to represent my house."

Even Colville was forced to recognize the dignity in the boy's voice, and he was sharply reminded that some day this lad would stand in place of his grandfather, and no one knew when that time might come. It might be wiser not to deal too high-handedly with him.

"Well, Edward?" The minister's voice was guarded but more genial.

"Sir, Mistress Barbara was under the protection of the house of Bruce. My grandfather is too sick to do anything to help her, but I do not think my father will be pleased when he returns from Edinburgh and finds she is a prisoner in the church tower."

Robert Colville frowned. "She is safer there than in the hands of the mob. That is why I suggested she should be lodged there and I should keep the key."

Edward's heart leaped at the mention of the key, but he kept the hand steady that held his hat. "But what will happen to-morrow?"

"Tomorrow, perhaps, your father will be home and he can then direct the matter, with my advice."

"But my father cannot be home till nightfall at the earliest. Down there in the town the wild ones among the salt-panners and miners are drinking themselves into a frenzy along the shore. They are lighting their furnaces again and vowing what they will do to the witch, as they call Mistress Barbara."

"They can do nothing while I hold the key," Colville replied.

"Sir, do you think those men will let the mere matter of a key stand between them and their victim? If you will not give them the key then they will come in force with their pickaxes and beat down the door."

Robert Colville looked uncomfortable. "They would hardly dare do that. They have more respect for my authority."

"I would not count on it too much," Edward warned him bluntly.

Hot anger mounted in Colville's face, but he restrained himself. "Doubtless a way will be found to satisfy the folk, yet bring Mistress Barbara to trial in Edinburgh. Remember she has been accused of witchcraft and poisoning, and witches and poisoners must account for their evil doings by death."

"You are condemning Mistress Barbara before ever she has been put to trial," Edward reminded him.

"And you speak out of your turn, young man, in an unbecoming way to your elders," the minister retorted, at last losing his temper. "There is no use in continuing this discussion. Go to your bed and leave such matters to those who are better fitted to deal with them." He pulled smartly on the bell rope and a bell jangled somewhere in the kitchen. Alison appeared.

"Show Master Edward to the door, Alison."

"Yes, sir," Alison bobbed.

"Have you taken those fellows their ale yet?" the minister asked.

"About an hour ago, sir."

"Good! You can bring my supper out of the oven again. Good night, Edward."

"Good night, Mr. Colville." Edward's voice was equally cold. Alison led him along the stone passage, bobbed a curtsy and closed the door behind him. Edward was so annoyed that he jammed his hat down hard upon his head. It was only when the key slipped out of the lining and bumped his crown that he was jolted to his senses and began to laugh.

"A mighty good thing the minister flew into a temper and got rid of me in a hurry," he told himself. He began to run down the hill.

Back in his study the minister kicked at the logs in the fire. "The impudence of the lad! But he is a Bruce, and the Bruces hold my living in their hands, so I must go warily. He might be right, too. It is difficult to deal with a mob when they get out of hand. Perhaps I should see that Mistress Barbara is conducted to some other place of safety? But how could I get her past John Horne and his friend in the porch?" Colville chewed his fingers, and glanced towards the desk where he had put the key, then shrugged his shoulders. "Well, there is no sense in letting my pie get cold a second time. While the folk are down on the shore drinking they will do little else. Barbara Ruthven will take no harm where she is for a few hours yet." He returned with satisfaction to his supper.

Edward reached Bessie Barr's Lodging by a roundabout

route, and dashed up the steps and tapped three times on the door. "Let me in! It's Edward!" he hissed.

As soon as the door closed behind him they asked eagerly, "Did you get the key?"

"Yes, here it is in my hat. Is the ale ready?"

"Aye, ready spiced and with the potion in it and heating in the little cauldron," Magdalen pointed to where it hung by a chain over the fire-basket in the hearth.

"Then we must get to work quickly. The mob is drinking down by the shore and once those people get worked up to a fury . . . ! Listen, Magdalen! Alison has already taken the guards a jug of ale. I heard her tell the minister so. When you take this jug, remember that."

"Yes, I will tell them the minister has sent them a second draught as the night is so cold."

"Suppose they do not drink it up at once?" James said with misgiving.

"They'll drink it right enough when it's hot," Isobel declared.

"I know a way to make sure it is drunk," Magdalen said. "Leave that to me."

"When you are sure and we have given time for the potion to work, then Isobel must show us the underground way into the church."

"We will all go up with Magdalen now as far as the ruined archway just below the minister's garden. There we will wait 'til she comes back to us," Isobel suggested.

They poured the boiling ale into the pewter jug. "It will have cooled enough by the time we reach the top of the hill," Magdalen declared. "I will carry the jug under my cloak in case we meet anyone. You carry the dark lantern, Isobel. We will go up by the narrow wynd. That is safer."

They reached the Tanhouse Brae without encountering anyone.

"That's a piece of luck," Edward said, as they left the last of the cottages behind them. Another two or three minutes and they crept into the deep shadow thrown by the ruined arch of the old monastery.

"I will come up the hill with you as far as the minister's garden while you go on with the ale, Magdalen. I can keep you in sight from there and hear what happens," Isobel suggested. She turned to James. "You and Master Edward stay here till we come back again."

The two girls went on up the hill till they reached the thick hedge round the minister's garden. Here Isobel motioned Magdalen to go on while she shrank back into the shadow of a tree. Taking a deep breath, Magdalen went on alone, the lantern in one hand and the jug in the other. When she reached the church door, she did not hesitate, but knocked boldly.

"Who's there?" came John Horne's voice from inside the porch.

"The minister thinks you could do with another tankard of hot ale, seeing it is such a bitter night," Magdalen called back, imitating Alison's clipped, high-pitched tones. "I've set it on the step. Drink it while it's hot, now, and set the jug on the step outside, if you want any more tonight. I'll be back for the jug later."

By the time John Horne and Thomas Bowman had got the bar lifted from behind the door, and the door opened, Magdalen was already disappearing into the darkness, the dark side of the lantern hiding her from their view.

"Why don't you stay and drink with us?" John Horne called after her.

"What? And have the minister coming to look for me?" Magdalen cried, apparently shocked. "It's more than my place is worth. Be sure and put the two jugs outside now, for you've got our other one in there too, and I canna bring more ale to you without a jug."

She heard the ale lifted in off the step and the door closed, then she reached the place where Magdalen was cowering in the hedge and with baited breath they both waited.

"Think you they'll drink it?" Magdalen whispered.

"Yes. I canna think John Horne will let yon hot spicy smell tickle his nostrils for long," Isobel gave a low chuckle.

She was right. Less than two minutes went by, then, with a clatter, the door reopened again, and John Horne stepped outside with two large pewter jugs in his hand. He looked down the road towards the minister's garden and both girls shrank back instinctively.

"There's no one about," he told Thomas Bowman. "The lass has gone back inside the house."

"Och, weel, just leave the jugs where she said!" Thomas Bowman gave a yawn. "I'm for a sleep in yon chair. Put the bar safely back behind the door. I'll give you a hand."

"Now!" Isobel said, rising to her feet. "Let's find the others."

CHAPTER 10

THE UNDERGROUND PASSAGE

THE boys were waiting anxiously in the depths of the ruined cloister court of the monastery.

"John Horne and the man with him have drunk the ale," Magdalen informed them and told of the proof. "How long will it take for the sleeping potion to work on them?" she asked James.

"About ten minutes usually. If we wait for fifteen minutes more, I think that should be safe enough," he whispered.

They sat on stones in the shelter of the wall's angle and waited. This was the worst time of all, to sit still and do nothing, when they were all impatience to find out what had happened to Lady Barbara. At James's heart was the grim fear that the shock and rough treatment might have been too much for her frail body, and he dreaded what they might find if ever they reached that top room in the tower. Isobel was watching the rising of the moon in the east across the Firth and its blurred reflection on the heaving waters. Her gipsy childhood had taught her how to measure the passing of time by the sun and the moon. At last she put a hand on Magdalen's arm and said, "Come now," and the three of them followed her a few yards down the slope to where a ruined terrace of rock and stone ran across the breast of the hill. She flitted along it till she came to a stone larger than the others that might once have been part of a broken pillar.

"Slip in behind this and follow me," she said, pushing back a stone like a paving slab. What had seemed but a narrow crack in the terrace wall widened out beyond the stone and the pillar. "Hold the lantern high," she directed Magdalen.

They were inside an arched tunnel with damp moss-grown walls that seemed to slope upwards. The floor was of slabs of stone. Soon they came to crumbling slimy steps.

"Watch your feet here," Isobel warned them.

Although the air smelled earthy and stale they had no

difficulty in breathing, for there seemed to be a draught of air from unseen inlets in the roof. Then the passage took a turning to the left, up another flight of stairs till it reached a final sloping passage that seemed to end in a couple of steps and a blank wall.

"Move as quietly as you can," Isobel cautioned them. "The church is just over our heads. Stand still for a minute and let us hear whether we can hear John Horne and Thomas Bowman talking."

With bated breath they listened, but not a sound was to be heard overhead.

"If they had been awake, we should surely have heard them speaking to one another," Isobel remarked. "This is the stone slab that leads into the church. Help me to push it. Put your weight on one side of it."

"We'll do that," Edward said. "You lasses stand back."

Edward and James pressed hard. The stone gave a little quiver then began to turn inwards on a central pivot. Another minute and a yawning gap appeared before them.

"I'll go first, in case there is danger. If you hear sounds of discovery, you and Isobel run away as fast as you can down the passage, Magdalen," James directed.

"I shall follow right at your heels," Edward hissed after him. "Turn and give me a hand up quickly when you are through the hole."

In a couple of seconds James had found his way up the narrow steps, little more than finger- and toe-holds, and through the gap into the church.

"Hand up the lantern," he whispered.

He shone it carefully round the floor, then in a slightly wider arc and found he was indeed in that part of the church known as the Bruce chapel; the very chamber where he had placed the casket in the wall. The thought of it gave him new courage as though his father watched over him.

"Is all safe, James?" Edward whispered from below.

"Yes. I am in the Bruce chapel."

"Then give me a hand up quickly." Another minute and Edward stood beside James.

"We have to make our way across the church now to the porch where those two fellows are sleeping," he whispered in James's ear. "The fewer of us who go stumbling about that porch in the darkness, the better. The lasses must stay where they are, in case of a fight."

Magdalen saw the sense of this. "We will wait here, ready," she promised.

"At the first sign of danger you must bolt down the tunnel and away, Magdalen," her brother warned her.

Magdalen said nothing, but there was a gleam in her eye that boded trouble if it came to a fight with John Horne.

"Come, Edward! We have little time," James whispered urgently. "There's no knowing how soon they might wake."

Edward took the lantern and led the way, splashing the light in a pool about his feet. James followed close behind him, his hands clenched. They went down two steps into the body of the church, then along to their right, to the inner door from the porch. Edward pressed down the wooden sneck of the latchet and held it firmly in his grip while he opened the door a couple of inches. From the two figures stretched out in the chairs came a rhythmic grunting sound.

"Listen to their snores!" Edward hissed, almost chuckling aloud. "It would take a cannon shot to rouse *them*!"

"Be careful all the same. So much depends on it," James breathed in a fever of anxiety. The perspiration broke coldly upon him.

Inch by inch they thrust the door open. Once it squeaked a little on its ancient hinges, and instantly both boys stopped dead, almost afraid to breathe, but the two sleepers in the chairs snored on. At last they were in the porch. They left the door wide open behind them, ready for their escape.

On tiptoe they picked their way over the outstretched legs and Edward chanced shining the lantern upon the door to the tower. The rhythm of John Horne's hard breathing faltered for a moment and they stood stock-still, but it recommenced and they let their breath go once more.

The boys hesitated no longer. With the key they opened the door to the staircase, and cat-footed they crept up to the top. Gently they opened the door to Barbara Ruthven's prison chamber. The woman lying on the floor gave a shuddering sob.

"Leave me! Leave me, I pray you!" she begged piteously. "I have done no wrong."

James was across the room in a trice and undoing the knotted

A yawning gap appeared before them

rope. "Aunt Barbara! Aunt Barbara! Not so loudly, please, for the love of heaven!"

She started up. "You, James! How did you get here?"

"Ssh!" He laid a gentle hand on her mouth. "You must make no noise. Your enemies are keeping guard in the church porch."

"I heard them!" Her body shook with fear. "They shouted insults from the door at the foot of the stairs. I was so afraid lest they should break it open and come up to me. They told me what they would do to a witch. Then they sang horrible songs."

James put his arm about her and comforted her. "Do not be afraid. They are asleep. There was a potion put in their ale to make them sleep. I cannot explain now. Edward is with me. He contrived to get hold of the key of your prison. We have come to take you away, but we must be swift and silent. You were always brave, Aunt Barbara. If you lean on me, can you walk down the stairs?"

"Give me a minute to chafe my limbs. I am stiff with the cold," she whispered. She rubbed her feet and legs, and then, with James's help, she dragged herself up unsteadily.

"Walk with me slowly round the room till I get the use of my legs again," she said.

With James on one side and Edward on the other, a step or two at a time, she moved about till the circulation was restored to her limbs again. Then she said quietly, "I think I might try the stairs now, but what of those set in the porch to guard me?"

"They are fast asleep. There is a chance that we may get you past them if we make no noise," Edward told her.

"But how shall we undo the great bar across the outer door without making a noise, and turn the key in the lock?" she asked.

"We are not going out by the door," James whispered, "there is another way—a secret way. Isobel Norrie and Magdalen are waiting there now. Keep your hand in mine. Edward will go first with the lantern. Keep your eyes fixed where he shines the light."

Edward led the way while James gave her the support of his arm. Down each stair they went, shifting the weight of their bodies cautiously from one foot to the other. At last they stood in the doorway to the porch.

This was the most dangerous part of all. The two boys had to help Barbara Ruthven over the feet of the sleepers. Just as they

were half-way to the other door John Horne stirred and muttered. Instantly they all froze into motionless statues. Then,
once more, John Horne's mouth fell open and the snores issued
from it.

Edward waved the lantern towards the door into the church.
"Now!" he urged.

They gained the church aisle and paused while Edward,
slowly and gently, closed the inner door into the porch.

"So far, at least!" he breathed.

Then, as swiftly as they dared tread with caution, they made
their way up the two steps to the Bruce chapel, where the lantern revealed the shadowy figures of Magdalen and Isobel
tensely waiting by the open hole in the floor.

"Thank God you have got thus far!" Magdalen breathed,
embracing Barbara Ruthven. "And now we have to help you
down that hole. Don't be afraid. It leads to a secret passage
that Isobel found, and comes out among the monastery ruins
on the hill-side. James, you go first to help her down."

It was not easy for Barbara Ruthven with her scarred limbs to
get down the hole into the passage, but she gritted her teeth and
closed her mouth tightly to prevent any cry escaping her. Between them, Edward and James lowered her gently, while Magdalen held the lantern to assist them. At last they were all safely
down in the tunnel again and Edward gently tilted the stone
slab. With only the dullest sound it settled into position again
above their heads.

Going carefully, but as quickly as they could, they reached
the end of the tunnel. At its mouth the moonlight threw a shaft
of white light over the frosty roofs of Culross. Before they
emerged into its full light, they stopped to consider their next
plan of action.

"Where shall we go?" James asked. "It is no use returning to
our home. That will be the first place the mob will search when
my aunt is found to be missing."

Magdalen had a sudden inspiration. "One place the mob will
never search is my grandfather's house. We must smuggle her
in there."

"But she might be seen by the maidservants," James objected.

"Not if we managed to get her into the spinning-room. No
one ever goes there at night," Magdalen declared. "It would
give us time at least to make other plans for her escape. Besides,

she needs food, and clothing, too, to replace those torn garments."

"Where can you get clothes without arousing suspicion," James asked doubtfully. "Remember her enemy Bessie Horne is within your house."

"Mistress Barbara also has a friend within our house," Magdalen said triumphantly. "There is my mother."

"Oh, Magdalen! We must not draw your mother into our trouble," Lady Barbara protested. "If it were found out that she had aided me, your grandmother would never forgive her."

"My grandmother will never know." Magdalen spoke with assurance. "All I shall ask of my mother will be clothing and money to help you. She will gladly give both, for I know she loves you dearly."

"Magdalen's plan will give us a breathing space," Edward agreed. "I have plans in my head too, for it is plain you must leave Culross as soon as possible if we are to save your life."

"But how am I to get into the spinning-room without being seen?" Barbara Ruthven asked.

"There is a door from the garden into the wool store behind the spinning-room. That is where the farmers leave the washed wool fleeces in sacks, you remember?" Magdalen reminded her. "The garden stretches up to the terrace below the cliffs. From there a flight of steps goes up to a door in the terrace wall, and that door gives on to the Narrow Wynd. Pray Heaven we meet no one on the way."

"From the noise, the folk of Culross are still carousing on the shore," Isobel remarked, looking down over the roofs to where fires were beginning to smoulder again under the salt-pans by the sea. "Pull your cloaks well about your ears in case we meet anyone on the way down."

"I will go ahead and make sure the door into the garden is unbolted," Edward said.

The others kept as much as they could to the shadows thrown by the walls and houses, but there were times when they had to cross the path of the moonlight. At one of these times, as they crossed the cobbled centre of the town by the market cross, a woman suddenly opened a door and called for her cat. She saw the little group and spoke to them.

"It's a bonnie night now. Are ye going down to see the big bonfire the folk are getting ready for the witch?"

The others were struck dumb, but Isobel had the wit to answer her. "Aye, Mistress Donald. Are ye no' going yoursel' to see the sport?"

"Na! I've a sick wean I canna leave, more's the pity."

To their relief the door was closed again.

At last they reached the lane known to Culross folk as "The Crown o' the Causeway", where the centre cobbles stood high above the gutters on either side, leading into the Narrow Wynd. The high walls here cast a deep shadow and they breathed a little more easily. Just over a hundred yards more and they reached the door into the garden. It was open and Edward waited by it.

"Go by the top terrace," he directed them. "Keep well within the shadow of the fruit trees and bushes that edge the terrace, for the moon is shining on the terrace, and you could be seen from the windows of the new house. When you reach the steps between the orchard and the vegetable garden, creep down behind the low wall there."

"Is the door open into the wool store, Edward?" Magdalen asked.

"Yes, I have seen to that."

"Then I will go there first. If there is no danger, then I will hoot like an owl and you can follow me. Keep in the shadow of the grotto at the end of the terrace till you hear me, though. Like a shadow herself Magdalen melted into the deep black shadows thrown by the trees. After what seemed an age of waiting, there came the unmistakable hoot of an owl.

"Quickly, now! Follow me!" Edward directed them.

Without discovery they reached the door into the wool store. Magdalen beckoned them on. "The maids are all in the kitchens below," she whispered. "Along the passage now and into the spinning-room!"

Once they were all inside the door at the head of the turnpike stair, Magdalen turned the key and waited till they got their breath again.

"I am going now to my mother," she said. "I hope I get her alone. I may have to wait for that, so do not be troubled if I seem a long time."

"And I have an errand too," Edward said. "I am going to see Andrew Brown."

"Will you stay here, too, Isobel?" Magdalen asked.

Isobel shook her head. "No. I can be of better use along the shore." They looked inquiringly at her. "I can hang about on the fringes of the crowd by yon bonfire and find out what those wicked ones are meaning to do. No one will be surprised to see me there, for my father's hut is down by the shore. If sudden danger threatens, then I can move quicker than the crowd and run and warn you of it. Leave the outer door on the latch."

"Lock this inner door behind us," Magdalen warned Barbara. "When we come back we will scratch like a mouse on the outside of it, so you will know who it is."

Barbara Ruthven and James huddled beside the dying embers still left in the fire, saying nothing at first. Barbara thrust out cold hands and feet towards the red glow. Two great tears rolled down her cheeks. James saw the glint of them in the firelight.

"Don't weep, Aunt Barbara," he begged. "We shall get you safely away from here, you'll see."

"I am not weeping for fear, James. I am weeping because the fine dreams I had for you have come to nothing, and I have brought you misfortune instead of happiness in Culross."

"Are you thinking of yon fine mansion up the hill behind the church?" James whispered.

She nodded miserably.

"Then the dream of that inheritance would never have brought me true happiness, Aunt Barbara. Put it from your mind, as I have done already."

"Have you, James?" She looked towards him with large inquiring eyes. There was decision in his voice, and it seemed as if he had grown from a boy to a man at one stride, a man who knew what he wanted of life.

She gave a deep sigh. "I wonder why, then, we came to Scotland?"

"There was my father's wish that his heart should rest at Culross," he reminded her. "I am not sorry that we came. It was as though I had to come here, that the way might be made clear to me, Aunt Barbara."

"What way, James?"

He frowned into the fire, clutching his knees within the circle of his arms, and was just about to answer when there was a quick stealthy step and a scratch on the door. It was Magdalen who entered. Her mother was with her.

"Barbara! Barbara!" Mary Preston whispered hoarsely, her

arms about Barbara Ruthven. "Oh, that this foul thing should be done to you! I have been praying, *praying* that my husband would return before it was too late."

"Mary, you did not believe I put poison in that phial to give Sir George, did you?" Barbara begged her.

"Indeed I did not! I would as soon believe it of myself. There has been some wickedness at work to bring you low, of that I am sure," Mary's voice rose a little with indignation.

"Ssh, Mother! We must not be heard," Magdalen warned her. "Here are the clothes, Mistress Barbara; a warm woollen dress and a thick cloak. Slip behind the door of the cupboard and put them on. I will hide your torn garments among the sacks of wool."

In two or three minutes Barbara Ruthven reappeared wearing Mary Preston's clothes.

"We are much of a height. You might be mistaken for me in the darkness," Mary exclaimed.

"Hush! There is someone coming," Magdalen whispered urgently.

This time it was Edward.

"I have been to see Andrew Brown," he said, relief in his eyes, "there is a Dutch boat which has been storm-stayed and which will leave on the full tide just after midnight. Andrew says the captain is trustworthy and he can persuade him to take you aboard, but it may need a little money."

Mary Preston plunged her hand into her pocket and drew out a beaded purse. "There is a gold piece and silver in this. It is all I have at present, but it might get you to Holland."

"I am grateful indeed, Mary. Some day—some day I shall hope to repay you," Barbara Ruthven said brokenly.

"There is no question of repayment between friends," Mary told her.

"Andrew will speak to the captain for you, but we shall have to hide you here till the ship is ready to sail when the tide is full," Edward said.

"How shall I get to the quay?" Barbara Ruthven asked. "I should have to pass by the Sand Haven and close to the salt-pans, and the folk there would see me."

"Andrew has a better plan for you to join the ship. He thinks it would be best to go up the coast road towards Kincardine. Less than a mile from here there is a fisherman's boat pulled up on the shore. When the tide rises he will row you down the Firth and wait for the Dutch ship to put out. He will arrange to signal the captain with a lantern for you to be picked up in mid-stream. But there are three hours to go yet."

"Then you must stay here till the time comes for you to go," Mary Preston insisted. "Settle yourselves down by the fire and get what rest you may. Magdalen and I will keep watch beside you."

Up in his house Robert Colville could not settle to go peaceably to his bed. He kept turning Edward's words over and over in his mind, and standing by his window he could hear the raucous shouts and the drunken singing of the crowd round the salt-pans. He began to have doubts about his power to hold these wild people in check, in spite of his words to Edward. If a mob like that went mad there was no knowing what damage might be done to his church, or what George Bruce might have to say on his return if the rabble had done harm to Barbara Ruthven.

Colville began to cudgel his wits for a solution. He could not let her go free himself, for he dreaded the frenzied wrath of the mob. Besides, the two guards were still sitting in the church porch. Perhaps it might be possible, under the pretence of Christian charity, to take food to Barbara Ruthven and to leave the key in her prison chamber and hint as much to her? He had no wish to help Lady Barbara, but he did not wish to be answerable to George Bruce for her death at the hands of the mob when they came storming up the hill to the church, as they surely would. It would be a different matter if they caught her in the open trying to make her escape.

He went to his desk, withdrew the drawer and felt at the back of it. The key was gone! He thought of the only visitor he had had that night. Edward! Black anger flooded his mind for a moment, then his brain cleared. If that was the way of it, then it might be for the best. He was relieved of all responsibility. But what had Edward done with the key? How could he get Lady Barbara past the guards? Overcome by anger and curiosity, he put on his cloak, took a stout stick and his lantern, and went to find out.

He knocked when he reached the church door, but it was not opened. Then he shouted, "John Horne! Thomas Bowman!"

but still there was no reply. Colville gave the door a number of heavy blows with his stick and at last he heard a sleepy stirring within. "What is it? What is it?" Horne's voice said drowsily.

"Your minister is here. I have come to see that all is well with you and your prisoner."

There was a muttered grumbling and cursing as John Horne roused his friend and they lifted the great bar from the door.

"Is that the way you keep watch?" the minister asked drily.

"We both fell asleep, sir," John Horne said sheepishly.

"That's plain! I thought I heard footsteps running on the hill and I came to see that all was well with you." He cast a glance over the lad's shoulder. The door from the porch to the tower stair was standing ajar! "Why, look!" he cried. "What is that door doing open? Your prisoner? Is she still in the room up the stair?"

Both men gaped open-mouthed.

"Run up, both of you, and find out. I'll keep guard here."

John Horne raced up the stairs with Bowman after him. The instant their backs were turned on him Robert Colville whipped the key out of the lock of the stair door and slipped it into the pocket of his cloak. The lads came clattering down the stairs again.

"She's gone! The room's empty!" Horne gasped.

"But how did she get out? Have you had this outer door barred all the time?" Colville asked sternly.

"Aye, sir, surely, except when the lassie brought us our meat and ale. Did we not unbar it to you ourselves?"

"Search the kirk!" Colville snapped at them. "If she did not go out by the door, then she must still be here."

Horne snatched up his smoky lantern, but though he and Bowman looked in every nook and corner, no sign could they see of Lady Barbara Ruthven.

"She's not here! It's black magic, that's what it is!" Horne told the minister.

"Look ye here, John Horne! The woman's vanished, and the only way to get out is by yon barred door in the porch. Are ye sure she did not give ye money to let her go through and to bar the door after her when she'd gone?"

John Horne began to shake with fear. "No, no, sir! I swear it! We have taken no bribe to let her go."

"There will be others besides me who will ask that question,"

Colville warned him sternly. "What are you going to tell your father and the other miners and salt-panners when they find you have let her go? She could not bar the door behind herself, you know."

Horne went pale and licked his lips in terror. "Sir, I know nothing about it."

Bowman also was quaking. "We were fast asleep, sir, when you came. You know we were! The witch must have put a spell on us to make us sleep."

"That's it!" John Horne cried quickly. "Why else should we both fall asleep like that? And strange terrible dreams I was having too."

"Oh, what kind of dreams?" Colville asked with interest.

"I thought I saw a great bat fly out from the top o' the kirk tower," Horne said, drawing heavily on his imagination.

"Guid sakes, man! That might have been the witch fleein' awa'!" his friend Bowman exclaimed. "She couldna get out any other way save through the door that was barred."

"No. She could *not* get out any other way except by the door, unless she took wings and flew, as witches can." Robert Colville gave time for the meaning of his words to sink in. "You will have to tell that to the folk in Culross making ready her trial, that she cast a spell of sleep upon you and in your dream you saw her fly away on her black wings."

"Aye, I'll do just that," Horne nodded. "The truth it is, too."

"It might be better if you went down the hill and told the folk yourself what had happened. They would more likely believe you than if you wait for them to come up here and find out," Colville said shrewdly. "Remember there are other witches who have been imprisoned in this tower, who did *not* get away. If you tell the folk of your own accord, you may persuade them you have had no hand in her escape."

"You're right, sir. Come, Tom! We'll go at once."

The two youths set off running down the hill. Colville laughed grimly when he saw them go; then, as he looked about him thoughtfully, he said, "Maybe it was better that way after all! All the same, Barbara Ruthven, I wonder how you did get out of this place, and yet leave the door barred behind you?"

When John Horne reached the crowd upon the shore, he dashed up to his father and grandmother. "She's gone!" he cried dramatically. "The witch is gone! She put a spell on

Thomas Bowman and me that we couldna stir hand or foot, then she flew awa' on great black wings." His story did not lose in the telling.

"Aye, aye! It's true what he's telling you," Thomas Bowman supported Horne's tale. "No man can stand up against black magic. We're lucky to get off wi' our lives."

"Ye feckless loons, to let her go!" Adam Horne cried, lifting his hand as though to smite his son, but Elspeth Horne pulled at his arm.

"Na, na! Dinna strike the lad. That'll no' help us to find the witch. Which way did she fly, lad?"

John Horne pointed vaguely westward.

"Aye, she'd fly awa' from the rising sun. But she'd no' fly far," the old hag said with cunning.

"Why not?"

"Yon lad she calls her nephew! D'ye think she'd leave him for long? No! She'll have told him where to find her."

"Think ye that, old Elspeth?" a man cried.

"Aye, I'm sure o' it. Get the lad and make him tell ye where she is. There are plenty o' ways o' making a young lad talk, even if he doesna want to do," she told them wickedly. "Fire to the soles o' his feet!"

A hubbub of talk broke out among the mob. "She's right! The lad could tell us where the witch is!"

"But he's a Bruce. There might be trouble if he's hurt."

"Och! If he's weel frightened, he'll speak."

"If we all take a hand in it, then no man can be blamed by himself."

"Get weapons, all of you! We'll seek him in Bessie Barr's Lodging, or demand him at the great house itself," Adam Horne incited them.

No one saw Isobel Norrie detach herself from the crowd and flit silently away. Once she was well clear of them, she ran her fleetest. Across the Sand Haven she fled, up by the steps behind Bessie Barr's well, and into the shadow the great house of Bruce threw across the garden. She slid breathless into the spinning-room.

"Mistress Barbara and James must get out of here at once," she gasped. "The salt-panners have found out that she has escaped from the church tower and they are coming to look for her in Bessie Barr's Lodging first and then here——"

"They would never dare to storm this house," Mary Preston declared.

"No, but they will crowd round the house, and Lady Bruce might turn her out from it. How will she reach the ship then? They are saying, too, that they will take James Bruce and torture him till he tells where she is."

"Oh, no, no!" Barbara moaned. "I will give myself up to them first."

"No need of that! Come with me quickly, both of you, and I will hide you in a place where they will never come. Come now! Now!" Isobel urged them. "Wrap your cloaks round you." She almost pulled them from the room. "Edward, when it is safe and it is time for them to go to the ship, come and whistle down the landward shaft of the Moat Pit."

"You cannot go down there! You'll drown!" Edward cried in horror.

"Leave it to me! Come quickly now. Run, Mistress Barbara. They must not see you."

Out through the garden they went, down the steps by Bessie Barr's well, and flitted round the gable end of the shadowed cottages. They reached the road. From the shore on the far side of the Sand Haven the roar of the rabble was growing, a horrible screaming, like a beast after its prey.

"They are not in sight yet!" Isobel panted. "Run for it across the road."

Like rabbits scuttling for cover they darted across the strip of moonlit road and into the shadow of the mine buildings, deserted and wrecked, the great wheel of buckets tipped at a crazy angle. Down between the banks of coal dust they ran till they reached the stone building over the mine shaft. There was an eerie sucking sound as the water rose and fell in the shaft with the lift and fall of the tide.

"We cannot go down there, Isobel!" James cried, drawing back in dismay. "There's no way down there now."

"Oh, but there is!" Isobel persisted. "After the mine was flooded I climbed down with a lantern to see for myself. I have no lantern now, but will you trust me and follow me in the darkness? There is a ledge where we can all hide and no man can come at us, save one at a time, and that at his peril."

"Lead us then, Isobel," Barbara said quietly. "It is our only chance, and drowning is better than death at their hands."

"After me down the ladder, then, and put your feet where I tell you."

Isobel went first, Lady Barbara next and James last, feeling for a footing on the slimy rungs of the ladder. Once James's foot slipped, but he clung with his hands and pulled himself back on the rungs again. As she went down, Isobel stretched out her hand and felt constantly at the wall of the shaft. They were within two or three yards of the water when Isobel stopped. "This is the place here," she said. "Can you swing yourselves to the right off the ladder on to the ledge? I will catch hold of your hand as you do it."

Sure-footed, she swung herself on to a ledge about three feet wide, then turned and caught Lady Barbara by the hand. "Step boldly to the right, now."

With a catch in her breath Barbara Ruthven did as she was told and found herself safe beside Isobel. Isobel handed her along a couple of yards and said, "Sit down, mistress. That way you cannot fall." Barbara obeyed her, then Isobel turned to the ladder again. "You now, James." She clasped him by the hand and he swung lightly towards her. Another moment and they were all three sitting on the ledge.

"It is part of an old working near the shore itself," Isobel told them. "The coal was taken from it long ago. I noticed it when I first came up and down the ladder with a lantern, and once I hid myself there when my family first began to work in the mine and I hated it. When they were all down the ladder, I scrambled up back again and out into God's sunshine, and climbed the hills behind Culross. A terrible beating I got from my mother afterwards, but the day under the blue sky with the fresh winds blowing was worth a beating."

"You poor child!" Barbara Ruthven said in compassion.

It was clammy cold down the mine and Isobel shivered a little.

"Come closer inside my cloak," Barbara urged her. "You have no cloak of your own. This is big enough for the two of us." Barbara placed half her cloak round Isobel and put an arm about her.

"But I am not clean like you," Isobel said.

"Better for us both to be warm, my lassie!" They huddled closer together in the cold darkness.

"If—if we get away," James said doubtfully, "will it be

safe for you to go back among your own folk, Isobel?"

"Have no fear for me. No one, except your friends, knows what part I have had in your aunt's escape, and they will never tell."

"You can no longer work in this mine, for the coal is deep under the water. What will you and your family do, child? Will they go a-gipsying again, think you?"

"Perhaps *they* will. I do not know. But I mean to stay in Culross."

"But why?" Barbara sounded surprised.

"When Magdalen and I were waiting for you in the darkness of the church, we whispered together about these things. Her mother needs a nursemaid for the little children and Magdalen said she would speak to her mother for me, if I wished it."

"And you do?"

"Why, yes. What greater joy can there be than to tend little children and to be near Magdalen? Besides, when we are together we can help each other to remember what you have taught us about herbs and healing."

Barbara Ruthven thought of how tenderly Isobel had brought the small children to her, to be helped and healed, and she pressed the girl closer to her.

They spoke little after that, just waited and slept a little, wakened and waited again. Slowly the stars reeled round the sky and the shadows shifted as the moon came round toward the west in a great arc. Then, at last, came a shrill whistle down the shaft. It was repeated, then they heard Edward's voice, "Are you all right down there?" in sudden anxiety.

They all started to their feet, but Isobel put out a hand to steady Barbara. "Do not move too quickly," she said. She called back up the shaft. "We're here. Is it safe to come up?"

"Yes. Andrew is with me."

"Wait till I come down with a lantern. I will help you," Andrew called to them.

A light gleamed on the dark water below. Then, with lantern swaying and bobbing, Andrew arrived beside them.

"This was well thought of, Isobel Norrie," he said. "None of the crowd would think you would dare to come down here."

"Have they gone now?" Lady Barbara asked, trembling a little.

"Yes. They ransacked your house, mistress, and despoiled it, but as you will not be going back to it, that cannot hurt you now. They went to the big house and demanded that James should be given up, and things looked ugly for a few minutes, but Lady Bruce did you a good turn there."

"But how?"

"She appeared at the head of the stone steps and asked them what they meant by making such a din before her house when her husband was lying so ill. One of the rabble asked her if she was concealing *you* in the house. 'No, I am not! Do you think I would take in a witch who has brought such great disaster on our house?' she replied."

The tears welled up in Barbara Ruthven's eyes. "I am sorry she thinks so ill of me. For her husband and her family I have nothing but friendship."

"Well her ladyship knows that! She is no fool, for she told them to go to their own houses and shut the doors, and that anyone who disturbed the peace of Culross would answer to her son next day. Then she spoke to Adam Horne, the ringleader, and singled him out. 'As for you, Adam Horne, go you home! Drink less, and keep your foolish family in better order,' she said. They went home like whipped curs. Then she turned to Edward and said in a low voice, 'You can tell Barbara Ruthven that I made the way clear for her, that she may go in peace,' and she went back into the house."

"I am thankful for that. Tell her some time, will you?" Barbara's face shone in the light of the lantern.

"Come now. Edward and Magdalen are waiting for us at the top of the shaft. You go first with the lantern, Isobel. I will help Mistress Barbara."

The little procession arrived safely at the top of the shaft, and Edward took Lady Barbara by the hand.

"Wait here till I make sure the road is empty," Andrew said. In a couple of minutes he was back. "Not a soul stirring! Not a light to be seen! Haste ye along with me."

They trod silently along the grass verges between the beach and the road. Soon the cottages of Culross were behind them, save for one hut belonging to a fisherman about a mile along the west shore.

"Old William Paton lives here. The boat down on the beach belongs to him. I have an arrangement with him that I sometimes take his boat out for a night's fishing, so he will not think it strange if he looks out from his window and finds the boat gone. But he is a sound sleeper and I do not think we shall disturb him," Andrew chuckled. "Help me to push the boat down into the water, boys." When the boat was afloat, he turned to Lady Barbara. "Are you ready now, mistress?"

Barbara turned to Magdalen and took her in her arms. "It is good-bye now, Magdalen."

"God go with you, Lady Barbara," Magdalen cried, weeping. "I shall never forget you, never!"

Edward took James by the hand. They looked at each other as they did when they first met, and they knew that as long as life lasted they would be friends.

"You will come back some day, James, when all this stramash has blown over?"

"Yes, Edward, I shall come back, but first I have many things to do and to learn. I will write to you and send my letters by ships coming to Culross, and if ever you have need of me, I shall come to you." It was as though they made a pledge to each other.

Then James shook hands with Magdalen and with Isobel, and Barbara stooped and kissed Isobel. The gipsy child put up a hand wonderingly to her face. "No one ever kissed me before, not even my mother!" she whispered.

Barbara Ruthven turned to Andrew and signed that she was ready. Andrew lifted her over the stern so that the waves did not touch her feet, then gave a hand to James. Edward helped to give the boat a slight forward thrust into the water, then Andrew climbed into the boat himself and thrust off from the shelving beach strongly with the blade of his oar. A few strong strokes and they were well out into the water. They waved to the three children standing disconsolate on the shore, then Andrew settled down to a steady rhythm of rowing that soon carried them into the strong current of the Firth. The tide had turned and was bearing them away to the sea.

A mile downstream the Dutch ship was anchored. A lantern was waved from the stern and Andrew headed the boat towards it. There was a quiet hail which he answered, "Aye, it's me, Andrew Brown, wi' your two passengers."

A rope ladder was let over the side, and Andrew steadied the boat while James assisted his aunt to climb. When they were safe aboard, they called down to Andrew, "Good-bye,

Andrew. We'll never forget what you have done for us."

"Good-bye, and God go wi' ye," Andrew called back. "Ye'll be sore missed in Culross. Haste ye back to Scotland when things are right for ye."

This brought great comfort to Barbara Ruthven.

The anchor was lifted and the captain shouted to his crew to hoist the sails. Billowing in the moonlight like a water-lily in full bloom, the ship began to move down the stream, away from Andrew in his lonely boat.

They bore away down the Firth, the shores widening to the great sea estuary. Barbara Ruthven and James Bruce leaned on the bulwarks and watched the land on each side fading into darkness, saying nothing to each other for a long time.

Then James asked, "Where is this ship bound, Aunt Barbara?"

"Save that it is Holland, I do not know." She called in Dutch to the man at the tiller, "Where do you make your landfall, sailor?"

"At the mouth of the old Rhine, near Leiden."

"Leiden!" she exclaimed gladly.

"Leiden? That is where there is a fine school of medicine and anatomy. Could we stay there, Aunt Barbara?"

"Why, yes, if you wish it." Her eyes were shining and she gave a strange smile. "Why do you wish to stay there, James?"

"So I can attend the school and learn from the professors there, of course. Aunt Barbara, now I can tell you, now it no longer matters about my inheritance in Scotland. I would rather be a doctor than the lord of the great mansion of Culross Abbey. I have heard tell there is a fine anatomist in Leiden. He knows more about the human body than any man alive. Perhaps I might study with him? I cannot remember his name, but would he take me as a pupil, do you think, perhaps when I am a little older?"

She laughed gently, a gay happy laugh. "Yes, I am sure he would. I can tell you his name, though it is not the one he goes by. He is William Ruthven, my brother."

"The one who escaped from England and the King's vengeance, and disappeared?" James's voice was full of wonder.

"Yes. He went to many universities, Padua, Vienna, Cologne, Leiden. Like Patrick in the Tower of London, all he cared about was to be a doctor."

"Aunt Barbara, even in his imprisonment I do not think my Uncle Patrick was unhappy, for he had leisure for his great learning. Like Patrick and William Ruthven, that is all I care about too, to be a doctor and heal the sick."

Barbara hugged him to her. "It lies at the heart of every Ruthven."

They stood watching the distant hills outlined against the westering moon.

"Farewell, Scotland! It is the end of an old song," Barbara said, the tears springing to her eyes. James faced her about, to where the boat was heading for the open sea.

"There is the beginning of the new song," he said. Already there was a glint of golden light in the grey of the east.